Some College Somewhere

Also by Joseph Anthony

An Uneaten Breakfast:
Collected Stories and Poems

———————

"Warm poetry and short stories make a pleasant combination. Captivating—keeps the reader on the edge of his or her chair."
—Bea Smith, The Local Source

"Using lyrical poetry and prose, Mr. Anthony adeptly weaves a map of the emotional landscapes within and between his characters. *An Uneaten Breakfast* resides strongly and comfortably among classic and contemporary masterpieces."
—Samsara Literary Magazine

The Alphabet of Dating

———————

"Will have you cataloging your own quest for love. Seasoned, crisp…and full of universal truths."
—Richard Polk, author of *Mantis Prayers* and
The Boarder on Monroe Street

"An intriguing tale of the nuance of relationships and the impact they have on us all."
—Linda Rawlins, author of *Sacred Gold* and *Fatal Breach*.

"Relevant…Innovative…Highly recommended."
—Samsara Literary Magazine

Some College Somewhere

Joseph Anthony

Published by Diamond Mill Press
184 South Livingston Avenue Suite 9-198
Livingston, NJ 07039
www.diamondmillpress.com
facebook.com/diamondmillpress

Some College Somewhere

The story "I Really Wish You Weren't" was first published by *Scarlet Leaf Review* in September, 2016. The story "Oliver" first appeared in issue 20 of *Samsara Magazine*. The Story "Echoes of Rubble" first appeared in the 14th print issue of *Five 2 One*, November, 2016.

ISBN # 978-0-9838745-6-0
Library of Congress Control Number: 2016959892

10 9 8 7 6 5 4 3 2 1

First Edition

Cover design by Joseph Anthony
Cover photograph by Alaina Belardo
Story title page artwork licensed through Shutterstock, Inc., all rights reserved to copyright holder: Baranovskaya

For my sister, Alaina,
who makes sure I never feel alone.

Contents

But Jesus said, "Let the children come to me. Do not hinder them! For the kingdom of heaven belongs to those such as these."

- Matthew 19:14

Aftermath, Beforemath

THE BLOOD IN MY VIENS feels as if it has been drained from me, spun in a centrifuge, purified, and returned to me while I slept. I can't remember returning to my apartment, but somehow I know where everything is. My arm reaches out until my hand finds the water bottle it is seeking. It can be deciphered by the minimal amount of pain in my eyes that I have not slept with my contacts in. Rolling from my stomach to my back, it feels as if my neck has disintegrated and my head might have spun off onto the floor, had the pillow not been here to catch it.

The nightlife around The University is a playground for children who miss their childhood—for those who need to escape reality at all costs. Some of us do manage to escape, at least until we wake up and pain mingles in where feeling has ceased, while the room keeps spinning—or stops spinning. Regret see-saws with sheer happiness as a conscious mind mixes with one that has escaped into oblivion and minute by minute as you lie there debating whether or not to move, you remember pieces of the night. Or maybe you can't. Either way most of us don't care because whatever happened happened.

Aftermath, Beforemath

And we know that there is nothing we can do to change it except close our eyes and go back to sleep.

AT THE FOOT OF MY BED there is an old brass chest on which folded blankets are kept. I can tell that the sun is high because of the glare it casts off the chest and onto the far wall by my closet. The blankets are tangled around me. This time I did not make it under the comforter. I ball the blankets up, throw them down to my feet, and kick them onto the chest to end the glare. There is no point in folding them if I am going out again tonight. Without the bright shine off the chest, the sun reveals other things in the room. There are fingerprints in the dust on the blank TV screen, which stands on the tall dresser by the closet. Each fingerprint tells a story of a small action that has been forgotten. Hands that had brushed up against its face by accident left more memorable traces than they may have known.

There is the shadow of giant wings on the floor. Turning to the windowsill, I see an orange butterfly with black spots pretending to be something much bigger than it really is. For a moment it has succeeded and I am moved by this phenomenon. How something so small can appear giant under the right circumstances. I stretch my legs, feeling hot, new, pain shoot from my ankle straight up to my hip. My jeans are hard and crackly by the knee and when I pull the material away from the leg itself, I can hear raw skin tearing from the dried blood. It is new skin, the skin that sits on top of a fresh wound, destroyed before it has the chance to harden and desensitize. Pain only lasts as long as it takes new skin to grow.

Alcohol is a wonderful thing, but painkillers—pain-assassins—are much more wonderful. They cut the leg off at the knee, for a short while, and replace the missing limb with a smile. All things in life are temporary. Pain, hopelessness, happiness, euphoria—all temporary. You can hold onto nothing longer than you are meant to have it. Our greatest happinesses, our greatest anguishes, are gone before they are fully recognized, and all that they leave is an intricate imprint on our memories to be deciphered in their aftermath.

There's a mirror on the ceiling, so I stare at my reflection, wondering how the young man high up there can look so much like me. *Fuck you*, I say to him as I roll over, but nothing changes in the picture on the ceiling. I reach up for him and he reaches back, locked in a staring contest that both of us refuse to concede. My arm drops back to the bed, lactic acid dissipating in the cool bed sheets, but his arm remains outstretched and nothing could be stranger. He's amazing. *How do you do that?* I wish he would answer. Smoke and mirrors, as is all magic. I'm charmed by his smile. There is something genuine about it, while at the same time, something different from anything I've ever seen before. I ask him to marry me, but before he can answer, I break up with him. My heart is already taken.

It is? he asks.

Oh, yes.

I'm too late then?

Yes. Much too late. It's too late for you and me.

It's too late for you and me.

Shut up.

Shut up.

Fuck you.

Fuck you.

He goes back to sleep and is gone when I wake up.

YESTERDAY IS THE SAME AS TODAY, and today is the same as tomorrow will be. There are beautiful prints of masterpieces by Rembrandt and Monet on the wall opposite my bed. These paintings were expensive, but I have enough money. I love to paint and to look at paintings—one of my only surviving passions—so they were worth it. Make no mind paying for something you love.

My phone is on the floor across the room, with a cracked screen and shattered camera, below a painting of the ocean. "Impression Sunrise." There is a hole in the sheetrock too misshapen to be from a fist. The necklace I am wearing is choking me, so I take hold of it and pull, breaking it into a thousand silver pieces. My feet are cold and the smell of my own body bothers me. Like a zombie, I roll out of bed. Begin stagger-walking to my phone with an urgency that I cannot explain. No one ever calls me. On my knees I pick up the pieces and with them clenched together between the dry lips of my mouth, I limp-crawl toward the bathroom.

As the water heats up, I stand and piss into the shower drain. The liquid leaving my body is gold and dark. As I watch it dilute in the water and disappear, I sit on the edge of the tub with my dick in my hand, thinking for a while about things I cannot remember. The tub begins to look more and more like a comfortable bed. The hot water soaks my clothes. The steam begins to clear my nose and I am thankful for the deep, unlabored breaths. I put my phone back together while I lay in the tub, but it does not work, the battery must be dead. Ivy comes to mind and I am in Italy. Grape vines and wine— fine wine. I vomit and the darkness inside washes away. No one is more successful at navigating the aftermath than I am.

Today everything is the same as it was yesterday. Yesterday longs for tomorrow but can never catch it. I can never catch it.

There is only yesterday for me.

With everything left in me, I push my pants to my ankles. Oh, the sweet smell of ivy. Laughter takes a firm grip on my shoulders and shakes me hard. My head bangs on the shower tiles. The ivy leaves turn white, like stars. Too many stars for any one person to look at for an extended period of time. My hand is sent on an errand to bring the bathmat between the tiles and my skull, but it never returns.

THE SHOWER CURTAIN IS MISSING. There is a warm, wet feeling between my legs that can only mean one thing. Looking down at the blanket shielding my body from the water, I find the curtain. Sometimes I surprise myself, a waterproof blanket in the shower. Who knows how long it's been since the last time I opened my eyes. The water is still running and the room is still spinning so nothing has changed. But something is different. I'm dehydrated and my leg begins to cramp. A phone starts ringing, but I am too tired to lift my arms and answer it.

"Hello."

It's not my phone. It's from the apartment next door. The walls are thin. They are thin and covered with tiny droplets of water, so I lick them. I lift my right hand to my face, brush the bangs away from my eyes with one finger. My tongue is willing to meet my hand half way as I pull the shower curtain towards my mouth, funneling water to my lips, licking it up like a homeless puppy until my leg feels better.

Some College Somewhere

As I lean over the edge of the tub, I find the bathmat in my left hand. I release it and stand up, removing the wet jeans from my ankles. All the while, the shower keeps running, the water beats down on my arms, awakening a numbness in every track mark.

My head is pounding. Bread, Tylenol, and more water, much more water, will help. It is difficult to take fast steps toward the kitchen without falling down, but closing my eyes helps me keep balance. *Do not take more than 8 caplets in 24 hours…*I've memorized the label long ago and it may be the smartest thing I've ever done. Still, I've found that taking more than 8 in 24 hours is okay, but I do not recommend taking more than 4 at any one time. I pour what looks like 4 caplets into my hand, taking them down with cold water, but I start to second guess myself. I may have just taken 5. Or was it only 4?

I sit down on the kitchen floor with my back against the cabinet and debate with myself for a long time. Soon, I decide that it's no big deal. The difference between 4 and 5 of anything really isn't that significant at all. It just means that they will need to wait for me a little longer than usual tonight, which they will do. They need my money to fill their needles, to fill their glasses and red cups. Yesterday will pick up where it left off, and we can forget about everything else in the world again.

———

Aftermath, Beforemath

THE SUN IS GONE. I'm not sure how I feel as I stand up from the kitchen floor, but I'm convinced that Tylenol is one of man's most underrated creations. My mind is clear and I don't realize I am smiling until I pass a mirror. I blink. He blinks. I touch the scar on my face. He touches the scar on his face. Each move he makes is like my own, but as I remember the last hallucination, it's clear that this is not always true.

I'm too late then?

Yes. Much too late.

The steps I need to take before going out again are clear, calculated, and meaningful. Clean up, then reset the stage. The first step is collecting the pieces of the broken silver necklace. I would like to throw them out because it is easier, but the pieces can be traded for pills. So I pick them up and place them in an empty prescription bottle. The next steps are replacing the shower curtain, which is easy, throwing the wet clothes in the hamper, which is also easy, and spackling the hole in the wall, which is only practical to do at the end of the week—because there will be more holes to fix tomorrow—and since it is not the end of the week, this is the easiest.

Follow these next steps exactly. Failing to carry out one of them could be fatal. Straying from a perfect routine is not recommended. I know that I can get drunk Matthew or high Matthew—or both Matthew's—through the return home. First, break the seal on two 16.9oz water bottles, taking one large sip out of each. If they are full when I scramble for them later, they will spill on my face. If they spill on my face, I may start to cough. If I start to cough, I may choke.

I take a new trash bag with handles, put it in the garbage bin, and place it down on the floor next to the water bottles at the side of the bed. The throw rug is already rolled up under the window. If it is left out, it may be thrown up on or tripped over. I reach out and twist the blinds so that they are more open. Allowing some sunlight to come through in the morning is vital for waking up and starting the recovery process again. Next, I throw out the old contact solution in my contact lens case and replace it. On more than one occasion I have lost contacts in my eyes while sleeping.

The most often forgotten step is turning my laptop off and placing the battery and power cord as far away as possible. This is the one thing that fucked-up-Matthew will forget if I hide them well enough. The passcode on my phone will also give me a hard time, keep me off the internet when I get home. Finally, I take basketball shorts and an old t-shirt and lay them on the bed for easy access, just in case I am coherent enough to change clothes, and I make sure to make the bed and fold a flap over so that I can see the sheets. This formula makes returning to the apartment as smooth as possible, as long as everything is done right beforehand.

My name is Matthew Rose. I was not always like this.

To stop caring about everything, you need to have once cared about something. There is peace in letting go, in giving in to the destruction. When there is nothing left to lose, there is nothing left to worry about. The moment I realized this, a huge weight was lifted from me.

Not every man is meant to survive a sinking ship. While every man may have a right to live, not every man is capable of saving himself. That is why only a few people, a few workable parts, may be pulled from the great destruction of the Titanic, or the little destruction of my cell phone. The only thing I can salvage from the wreckage is the sim card. He is my refugee, and it is my job to find him a new home. I pick a box off the top of the stack of new phones in the corner of my closet, cut the tape away from the edges, and assemble the pieces with a mechanical precision that frightens me. Everything ends as it begins.

There is no exception to this.

Oliver

WHEN I WAS A LITTLE BOY, my father used to take me to an overlook near our house. It was a reservation on top of a mountain with a stone balcony that looked down on a forest into the valley. The New York City skyline was visible from it and in the winter when there were no leaves on the trees, the buildings stretched all the way from left to right as far as the eye could see, curving with the world. It was beautiful when the sun set and the jagged, concrete horizon seemed to glow like red embers at the end of a camp fire.

"How many buildings are there in New York City?" I asked my dad.

"More than anyone will ever be able to count, son."

"Really?"

"Yes, sir."

"How do you know?"

"I've tried before, son."

I loved the way his eyes seemed to shine when he looked at the fiery buildings. There was something so subtle about his smile when he looked at that skyline. My best guess is that what I was seeing for the first time was

Oliver

15

contentment—one of the world's supreme treasures visible in the way the corners of his mouth rose.

Years later my mother would tell me, "He wanted to fill you with hope and make you curious about the world, Matthew."

These were his gifts to me: Hope, which is everything. And curiosity—a precious thing for a child because with it comes the search for answers and the birth of dreams.

"Tell me what you're thinking," Dad asked while we sat on the park benches near the edge of the wall.

"Try to guess," I told him.

"I think you're wondering how high the tallest buildings are."

"You're good."

He put his arm around me.

"Well, how tall are they?"

"Which ones, son?"

"That one there," I said, pointing.

"Ah, the Empire State."

"The what?"

"The Empire State Building. It's one of the most famous buildings in the world."

"Really?"

"Uh huh."

"How tall is it?"

"About a hundred stories."

"How tall is that?"

"Imagine fifty of our houses piled." He motioned one hand on top of the other, then slid his arm back over my shoulder. In that moment, I felt stronger than any building. As if my insides were built of steel and concrete, and that I would live forever in this world. I wrapped a small arm around his waist, rested my head on his bicep, and lost myself in what was left of the sunset.

"Matthew," he said.

"Yeah, Dad?"

"I'm so proud of you."

I WAS TOO YOUNG TO REALIZE just how much it would have meant to him if I told him that I was proud of him, too.

It was something his father never did, and something I often took for granted.

The man ran through walls of fire for a living. Motivated by a sincere care for other people—one which I still do not understand—to be a good man.

Of course, I was proud of him.

I never had any trouble hugging or kissing him in front of other people. Instead, I looked forward to those moments because I knew that I had something that many others would never have: a dad who went out of his way to give me affection, to tell me that he loved me.

Until the sunny Tuesday morning when bodies rained from a cloudless sky and black smoke rose from the depths of hell. I was sitting in social studies class when I began to notice the parents coming one after another to take their children out of school in the middle of the day. I thought to myself, *what lucky kids*, because they got to leave school early, but the depths of their real luck, I could not yet comprehend. I watched the shaken faces of adults and the confused faces of children as they walked hand in hand back to cars that would take them away.

That's when the rumors began to circulate. Nasty ghosts of thought that crept in and out of our ears, left us unsure what to believe.

Someone said that a bridge had fallen. Someone else said that the Twin Towers were gone. And then, with a sick sense of importance, our sixty-year-old emphysemic teacher said, "That's right, the Twin Towers are no more."

It was like hearing the news that you only had a few months to live from a doctor that had failed her course on bedside manner. There was no gentleness in her croaky voice. She made no effort to break such incomprehensible news to us with delicacy. The Twin Towers were gone, and it was nothing more than another historic fact to her, one that she seemed proud to have lived long enough to see.

My mother came for me in the middle of last period.

"He'll be alright," I said.

And when she brought me home and mumbled, "I hope so," I knew that he may be gone.

"You saw the traffic in the city on the news," I offered, but it wasn't enough. From then on, nothing would ever be enough.

Our old house was on a hill that faced the skyline. From our front porch, my mother and I could see the black smoke rise above the trees. I sat a step below her. She cradled me between her arms and legs, and began to cry with her cheek on top of my head.

"His department is only blocks away from the Trade Center. Every fireman in the city has to be there," she said.

"We just have to wait. We'll wait here until he comes home."

I was eleven years old and trying my best to be strong for her, but whatever I said only seemed to make her cry more. She didn't believe what I was saying.

I believed it though. There was no way that he could be gone. He always came home. It didn't matter if it rained. It didn't matter if he needed to jump from a second-story window with an unconscious victim in his arms. It didn't matter if he got heat stroke and we needed to pick him up at the hospital. He always came home.

For two days we waited on that front porch, uncertain about a certainty.

My mother had always begged my father to work closer to home, but he had grown up in the city. His father and half-brother had worked with the same fire department before joining the army. It was my father's greatest goal, to earn my grandfather's praise.

And then, on the third day, we saw it. A black SUV with a thick blue stripe pulled up the hill, and we both knew it would stop at our house before it ever turned into our driveway. A policeman that neither of us had ever seen stepped out and donned his hat. Dozens of hot spiders fumbled around for their legs inside of my chest, and when I took a step forward they scrambled up my neck and down my spine.

My mother rose but could not walk. Her fingers wrapped around the railing on the stairs so hard her hand turned white.

All of a sudden, I was desperate for the uncertainty again. Horrified by the finality of what was about to happen, I longed to be unsure, missing the hope I had taken for granted just moments ago.

"I'm sorry," the policeman said, removing his hat. "Mrs. Rose?"

"Yes."

"Your husband perished at the World Trade Center Tuesday morning."

My mother's knees buckled. Somehow, I found the strength to catch her. The officer helped me ease her into a porch chair.

"But maybe he's still alive," I went on. "Maybe he's just missing somewhere."

"His entire firehouse was lost in the South Tower collapse."

"You're wrong," I said. "He'll come home."

"Your husband was a brave man and a hero," said the officer, turning from me back to my mother, fatigue lacing his voice. "I know my words will mean little, but perhaps there is something in knowing that his actions helped save the lives of others. Please forward the information of your husband's wake and funeral. I'm obligated to give you a number that offers counseling, but I feel that most people will need to find their own way through this."

After apologizing again, he handed my mother a business card and left. The two of us made it just inside the front door before we collapsed together on the floor, clutching all either of us had left.

"TAKE AS MUCH TIME AS YOU NEED, Matthew," the principal of my school told me.

He'd come to see me at my house when he heard what had happened, it felt strange and out of place.

"I've spoken with your teachers. They'll do everything they can to make sure you don't fall too far behind. Don't worry about the work you miss."

For some reason, this was a small relief in a field of grief. It made me cry right there in front of him. He held me and seemed to understand.

But even with his help, I missed the honor roll for the first time in my life that marking period.

After she pulled herself together enough to drive, my mother took me up to the overlook. As she put the car in park, a huge lump rose in my throat. This time neither of us was crying. Instead, we just looked. Pictures of missing persons wallpapered the trees. Wax candles had melted into wax puddles on the sidewalks. American flags flew over the balcony and lay draped over benches and branches, wavering like unseeable spirits that were all too real and far too noticeable.

Strangers grieved in one another's arms, comforted to find others to share their pain with, and there was nothing strange about it. We were all trying to cope with the fact that whoever it was, was gone forever. That we would have to spend the rest of our lives missing them, clutching fragile memories.

Between two trees, a sign read: *Do not fear the tomorrow after Death, for Death's greatest fear is you looking bravely on that tomorrow.*

Gone but not forgotten was scribbled on cardboard and nailed to a picnic table bench.

It was all as one would expect. The overlook had become not just a shrine of patriotism, but an open, bleeding wound of red and blue for the murdered. And there were many others like it throughout New Jersey.

And then, like an afterthought, there was something different—something I was certain no other overlook or memorial had. To the far left, sitting on the edge of the wall with the city to his back, was a man with one arm playing the guitar.

Gone but not forgotten are we?
Darkness pulled from sunshine that again we'll never see.
They ask me if I've seen worse on the battlefields of 'Nam,
Been trying to escape the guerrillas, but here they come again.

He sang in a cracked voice while resting the guitar against his nubbed arm, which was bleeding through its dressings. I wondered how old or how new his wound was. He paid us no attention, just kept strumming the same off-key chord with his only hand.

To my right there were dogs growling. Coyotes playing tug-of-war with something. They pushed each other across the lawn, grabbed things people had left behind, ate things that were and were not food, looting like Nazi soldiers. All at once, I noticed the abundance of destruction and wanted to leave.

"I will always keep you safe, Matthew." My mother stopped me as I turned back toward the car, squeezing me to her chest. We would return here for all of our remaining September 11th's together.

THE FOLLOWING SUMMER, before seventh grade, my mother enrolled me in an art class.

"I think it would be good if you found a way to express yourself," she said.

As part of the deal for going, she agreed to buy me a skateboard so that I could go to the new skate park on the other side of town with my friends.

"Okay," she said. "I'll take you to the mall and we'll buy you whatever you need."

"Thank you! I promise I'll do anything you need around the house—anything."

"You're a good kid, Matthew. Don't worry so much, honey. Go out and have fun. I want you to have fun. That's all you need to promise me. That and sticking with the paint class for at least a month, give it a real chance and you might like it." She kissed my forehead.

"Okay, I will," I said, kissing her back.

So that afternoon, she picked me up from school and we drove to the mall.

We were stopped at a red light watching school buses follow each other through an intersection, each branching off toward a different section of town.

The light turned green and we headed straight. From the right, a car ran the red and t-boned us. Tunnel vision took over, slowing down time to an almost unbearable crawl. The front passenger window cracked the way car glass cracks—it broke but the pieces somehow held together, as if the fragments were holding hands. I lost track of my arms as I watched the door to my right bend inward until it reached my leg, kissing it until the pleasure of being kissed morphed into a sadistic needle prick that would not end. It stopped just before it snapped my femur. The scenery outside of the windshield began to rotate as the car spun around in a graceful pirouette. My head snapped forward. My eyes widened to the point of dizziness as I waited for an airbag that would never come. The seatbelt struggled to do all it could, and my body bent at the waist causing my face to hit an unforgiving jagged doorframe where the airbag should have been. It was then that I found my arms.

There was a loud crack in my ears as the driver-side airbag deployed, breaking my left arm at the elbow, which had reached across my mother's body. I found my right arm flailing out, in search of the emergency break, but the scenery had already stopped moving. My face felt loose. Hot pain flooded me. Tingling consumed my entire body as my senses were overwhelmed with too much information. Temporary blindness. Brief loss of consciousness. Ear-piercing screams woke me a minute later along with the sound of sirens. I thanked God that my left ear was going numb from my mother's screams. When I turned to look at her, I saw her head resting on the airbag as if it were a pillow. As she turned to look at me, I realized that I, too, was shrieking. Her glasses had vanished and she bled from both nostrils. With both of her hands still gripping the steering wheel, she lifted her head toward me and began screaming even louder.

"Nooo! No! No! No! Nooooo!"

The sirens grew louder, overtook her screams.

"Your fa-ace, Matthew!...No! No! No!"

With all of the energy she had left, my mother removed one of her hands from the steering wheel and reached as far as she could toward my face. Her breathing became short and her body convulsed as it began to shut down.

Shock, I mistook for a heart attack. I found her hand, supporting my broken elbow with my other palm, and tried to squeeze her fingers between mine.

The rearview mirror hung loose, looking at me like the devil, quiet and coy. I saw the dark red on my face—blood gets darker the deeper a wound goes. That's all I saw. With hot, stinging cheeks, I broke my gaze from the mirror.

"Stay with me...please keep breathing..." I blew her kisses..."Please, Mom. Keep breathing."

———

A CAST AND THIRTY STITCHES LATER, I was sent to recovery. My elbow would regain full range of motion, but the plastic surgeon could only do so much with my face. The sharp metal of the indented doorframe had cut me from just below my right eye all the way below my bottom lip in a crescent moon-shaped curl.

"The scar may fade over time, but it's going to be noticeable," the surgeon said to me. "You're lucky to not have lost an eye. I've never seen anyone so lucky and so unfortunate as you."

I tried to focus on the more important news.

"The doctors said that if we hadn't had the accident, they may never have discovered the cancer," Mom said.

During tests they had discovered a malignant tumor on her liver.

"We've caught it early enough," her doctor explained to us, as if the faster he spoke, the better the news would sound, "We estimate the survival rate to be over fifty percent. We'll need to go in immediately to remove it, but we should be able to get all of it, and the liver is the one organ in the body that regenerates."

It's difficult to remain positive when a fifty-percent survival rate is good news, but my mother was stone-faced. She had to be, for me. When you're looking down the barrel of a loaded gun, your own safety is not what matters to you. Instead, you think of your family—

or what's left of it—and how they will carry on when you are gone.

In the days leading up to and following the operation, she was fearless. She was strong during the months of chemo and through the loss of her hair, and it wasn't long before her cancer was in remission. Shreds of normality were returning.

One morning, with mischief in her eyes, my mother woke me up and told me to get ready.

"I'm taking you to that skate park."

Several of my friends were waiting downstairs, each holding a wrapped box. All at once, they handed me presents, looking no less excited than my mom to have surprised me.

One skateboard, new pair of shoes, and protective helmet later, we were on our way to the skate park. It was an outdoor arena of pipes and ramps. On the far right side, adjacent to the parking lot, was a pro shop. From the glass windows of a restaurant above the shop, several parents could be seen eating cheeseburgers while they watched their children tear it up below. On more than one occasion, I would hitch a ride to the park with one of my friends, look up toward the restaurant and see that my mom had snuck in to watch me.

We got halfway through the parking lot when something horrified me. None of the other boys were wearing helmets. My friends, who had all been to the park before, had failed to mention this.

"Mom?" I rolled my eyes at the helmet.

"Fine," she said. "Just be careful."

For hours and hours we kept skating. Fueled by the unnatural desire to jump from anything high, we pushed our bodies further than we thought they could go, reached heights we never thought we could reach. The aches felt so good the next day, the healing of broken down muscle into something stronger.

The skate park played music outside, a continuous loop of tracks that sounded more and more alike each time we visited. One day, during a lull between songs, an old man pulled into a handicapped parking space and limped through the admission gate. He wore a tie-dye shirt and carried a skateboard in his left hand. His hair was long and gray, pulled into a ponytail that hung halfway down his back like a rope. The whole time he walked, he appeared off balance, on the verge of falling forward. And then, something remarkable happened. He got to the lip of a bowl, jumped on his board, and road like nothing was wrong with him.

Anything was beginning to seem possible again.

When he stopped riding, I went over and offered him a Gatorade.

"What flavor is it?" he asked.

"Blue."

"Blue as a flavor? Who'd of thought?"

He took the drink and broke the seal, sipped it long and slow and seemed to enjoy it.

"What happened to your leg?" I asked.

"Work accident," he said. "Fell from a ladder."

"A ladder? Were you a fireman?"

The man shook his head, unwrapped his ponytail and set the Gatorade down on the bench between us. "Nope. I'm a painter."

"A real painter? Like an artist or you mean walls and houses."

A smile crossed his face and I wondered what was funny.

"I just love to paint," he said.

He closed his eyes, leaned back on the bench, warming his grizzled face in the sun.

At the risk of disturbing him, I chanced another question. "How can you skate with a bad leg?"

This got his attention. All at once his eyes animated with the urgency of a message. "Look right here, little dude. Every one of us has a bad leg."

I considered this, was about to ask another question when he continued, "The trick is to keep your bad leg on the board and let your good leg do all the work."

From then on, we were quiet. With one foot, he slid his skateboard back and forth, appeared to rock himself to the brink of sleep. I left him there, to his thoughts and perhaps his dreams.

Whenever I paint or drink blue Gatorade, I remember him.

"I DON'T WANT YOU TO REMEMBER me this way."

"You already know you can beat this," I tried to rally her. "We can beat this together."

"I know," she said, but there were fragments in her voice. A slight change of tone that told me she was resigning, looking for permission that I was incapable of granting her.

"We'll do everything we did before. And we'll keep eating right and exercising. You'll get better again."

"Yes. But, Matthew, if I don't get better..." tears leaked from the corners of her eyes like helium out of a balloon. "If I don't get better, I want to know that you'll be taken care of."

The only noble thing about cancer is that it does not discriminate. It attacks everyone: men, women, children, black, white, gay, straight, old, and young. It comes with an insatiable hunger, and it can never be trusted not to return. Yet still, cancer is capable of mercy. It not only takes lives, but it threatens and spares them, too.

For almost a year and a half we held onto hope that cancer would spare us. And each day my mother died a little more as I held her in my arms and rocked her to sleep.

People have children so that they can watch them grow, so that they can teach them things, so that they can experience many of life's greatest things together. But perhaps the more secret reason for having children is so that they can help ease us out of this world when our time comes. We have them so that they can hold us close as we drift further away toward oceans of uncertainty that slip through our fingers when we try to grasp them.

Everyone wanted to help, to hang out, to act as if nothing was happening, but I just wanted to be left alone. I needed to cherish every moment with her. The last big thing we did together was take a trip to Italy. We spent a week there seeing immortal works of art. Walking the same ground as millions had before us. She wanted to touch everything, to hold things in her hands and leave her fingerprints in places. I spent my time throwing Euros into what I imagined to be sacred fountains, making wishes that somehow made me cry and brought me hope.

In a corner of the Sistine Chapel, when no one appeared to be looking, we lay down on our backs and looked up as Michelangelo had once done.

"Look at you, Matthew. The same as the greatest painter the world has ever known."

I turned to her, took a sideways memory that I will keep with me for the rest of my life.

"Promise me you'll never lose that passion," she said. "Paint. Do things. Live."

A man came over and in broken English informed us that we could not do that. That we must stand if we wished to remain in the chapel.

So we left to have lunch at a rustic place just outside the Vatican City walls. Mom ordered a bottle of house wine, and to my surprise, the waiter brought two glasses.

"But I'm not old enough."

"I'm with you. It's fine, Matthew. One glass of wine is fine." She picked up one of the glasses, handed it to me as if she was presenting me with an award.

"How does it taste?" I asked.

"Let's toast and find out." She poured and I held my glass up to hers. "To fulfilling dreams. Because being here is a dream come true for me!"

It was then, as I had my first drink, that I realized all parents were kids with dreams once, too. Before they had children—not too long ago—they were young. And while it may have appeared to me that they always knew what to do, they had to figure everything out as they went along. As their kids grow up, they grow old. As they are teaching their children to chase after whatever aspirations they may have, they are busy learning how to give up on their own dreams.

After we returned from Italy, my mother began sleeping most of the day.

A month before it happened, she called me into her room, sat me down on the bed next to her, and began saying terrible things.

"There are some things I need to tell you, Matthew, and I need you to really listen. Your father's life insurance was $250,000. The day after we knew that he would not be coming home, I took an even bigger policy out on myself. When I'm gone, I've made arrangements for the house to be sold. You'll live with your uncle. I know you don't like him, but sometimes we don't like the things that are best for us."

I sat speechless at her bedside, unable to see what she saw, unwilling to acknowledge the end, hoping that closing my eyes would delay it.

"Your father needed to have the insurance because of his job. I never worried about myself, because I always knew if anything happened to me he was more than capable of raising you on his own. I took out the life insurance on myself so that you would be okay if anything ever happened to me. You won't be able to touch a penny until you're eighteen. When all is said and done, you will have close to $930,000, Matthew. We will always take care of you."

She held my hand in hers and for the briefest moment I thought everything might be okay.

I was fourteen years old when they laid her next to my father's empty coffin, and added her name to the headstone she and I had picked out for him.

I was alone in the world. A modern day Oliver with the twist of being force-fed a silver spoon.

Echoes of Rubble

W E WERE SITTING ON THE EDGE of the world holding one another, she with her hand down my pants and I with mine up her dress.

Two weeks after my sixteenth birthday, I went up to the overlook with Kaylee. The skyline of New York City would see everything, would smile on us.

"Are you sure you're ready?"

"I'm positive now."

"What makes you so sure?"

"I can see a future when I look at you," I said.

She pressed me up against a tree in the park, kissing me, telling me with her lips still pressed to mine that she thought she loved me. I had been thinking of this for a while now, but I wanted to be sure, because some things in life are permanent. When she told me that she understood, I believed her. Kaylee was genuine like that. Kaylee didn't care that everyone else would have been cruel to me if they knew that I had been the one stopping something like that from happening for weeks.

"And you couldn't see it before?" she asked.

"I wasn't sure if I was looking at the future or something else."

With my eyes closed, I kissed her, ran my fingertips up and down her ribs. Her mouth curled up at the sides to laugh, but I pinned her smile with my lips.

"Matthew," she said, "there aren't many like you."

We each learned a great deal in the next few minutes, most of which we were expecting, but some of life's greatest things catch us off guard—little secrets that seem to have always been there, hovering in the air around us, just out of reach until they permit themselves to be discovered. There was completeness to the moment that was humbling. We were communicating every thought without speaking. She heard me say how thankful I was that she had waited, through my deep sighs. She expressed you're welcome by briefly closing her eyes.

Far too few people experience something so meaningful.

"I think I love you."

But she moved away at the end of the summer, before I had the chance to say the words back.

My uncle thought it was hilarious.

"Sad because your little girlfriend dumped you?"

"She didn't dump me."

"Sure looks like she did."

"She moved away."

"To get away from you," he laughed. "Too bad though. She was a pretty little thing, tight little ass. Reminded me of the girls I used to go around with. Of course, I knew how to keep them."

This was when the only things I seemed able to hold onto were memories.

VERONICA WAS THE MOST beautiful girl who ever liked me. So beautiful, in fact, that I gave up smoking for her.

"I just can't stand the smell," she told me.

"But I am not a quitter," I joked.

"Well, maybe you should be. It might be good for you to just let go."

She was much too sure of everything for me to ever trust her. There was a confidence to her personality that demanded respect.

"It's just my Crazy Latina blood," she would say. And I would like her more for her modesty.

She always got what she wanted, but she was never a bitch about it. Of course, all the boys were crazy about her. For the life of me, I still don't know what she saw in me.

I thought that if I gave her everything she wanted—roses, jewelry, heroin—she'd keep coming around every night to rescue me from the loneliness.

This, of course, was back before I knew that trust is everything and I knew we had none of it.

Even in those last days, I didn't realize that I was pushing her away.

In the movie theatre, I slid my arm across her shoulders, and she fidgeted in her seat.

"You are so beautiful," I whispered in her ear, and she rolled her eyes.

Back at her apartment, she said, "You can come in if you want."

And I knew what that meant.

On my way out, while I groped around in the dark for my clothes, I told her, "This can work if we let it."

"Matthew," she said, pausing.

An ambulance tore through the streets of her run-down neighborhood and for the first time, I knew that I was in trouble. I could see her irises lit up by the street lamp outside her window, and mistook it for a glint of hope.

"I think I love you," I said.

That's when she went batshit.

Unleashed the Crazy Latina on me.

If you ever want to piss a girl off, tell her that you love her when you are both certain it isn't true.

MY UNCLE WAS A PERVERTED old man and a legend in his own mind. Once upon a time, he was a high school football celebrity. And while glory fades, vanity lingers. He was my father's half-brother—same mother, different fathers—and he was a full twenty years older than my dad.

"She probably didn't like your face. What girl would want to kiss a face with a big ugly scar on it?"

Half an uncle, half the blood, I would remind myself. *Kaylee moved away. It wasn't because of me.*

When I had first moved in with him, after the lawyers liquidated everything and froze the money, the old man went out of his way to be nice to me, but it was obvious that he didn't give two shits about me and was only after my money. He tried to get me to change my last name to his. My dad's father came from Roses, and my uncle's father had the last name of Klein. The day I turned eighteen, I went out and got "ROSE" tattooed in bold on my right forearm to make it clear where I stood.

But before I turned eighteen, I had to be respectful of him, because what choice did I have? He was still my father's half-brother, and I lived in his house. But I had very little respect for him as a man. He must have known this because he began trying to beat respect into me around the same time I met Kaylee. The man may have been old, but he was still bigger and stronger than me. He would be waiting with his Clint-Eastwood-face for me to get home from school, and as soon as I walked through the front door, he'd start wailing on me with his four-fingered fist.

"Fire!" I would yell, "Fire! Fire! Fire!"

My father told me once to yell *fire* if I was ever in trouble because "People never come for help, they always come for fire."

The front door wouldn't even be closed half the time, and he'd be there pounding away at my ribs until the wind was gone from my chest and I couldn't scream anymore.

No one ever came.

With all the money I could stuff into my pockets, I ran away one night and figured I was leaving behind a life I was never meant to live. Sixteen is too young for a boy to live on his own, but I had been on my own ever since my mother died. I bought a one-way train ticket south and stayed for a few days in a rundown hotel, hiding out among crackheads, hookers, and illegal immigrants. Soon, I ran out of money and went back home even more dejected than when I had left.

It's depressing running away from a house where no one is looking for you, where no one is calling you back.

IT WASN'T ALL BAD ALL THE TIME with Veronica. There were times when we were good together. We were at our best in Atlantic City, where we were walking down the boardwalk at three in the morning, both of us wired on coffee and booze, inspired by the bright casino lights.

All the night creatures were out. Some scary shit that reminded me of The University on its best weekends.

"Love me!" a woman yelled, stumbling after a large bald man in the sand to our left.

One of the woman's heels snapped. She fell face first into the sand, and when she pushed herself up, grains of it stuck to her lipstick and made her look trashy. As she chased after him, her silver dress sparkled like the ocean. The man held her away with a stiff arm as she scratched at him, and even through the multi-colored lights, the blood was visible.

There was nothing she could do to hold onto him.

"Love me! Please, love me! Why won't you love me?"

Soon, Veronica and I were out of ear range.

"Puta. Hooker," Veronica said, but I wasn't so sure. I'd seen just a little too much desperation.

At a snail's pace, we walked back to our room at Harrah's.

As we made our way, the city came to life for us. It breathed with us. It told us its dirty secrets with every gum splotch we saw on the sidewalk, with every empty can we took turns kicking, with every moist condom we stepped over.

Atlantic City can best be described as The City of Almosts. You almost leave with more money than you came with, you almost have a good time and feel hap-py...you almost fall in love.

As we made that journey together, she let me car-ry her on my back. We shared a jacket because she had left hers on the back of a slot machine chair. We grew tense at every person we passed on the street, expecting to be mugged or roughed up by someone who had been less lucky than we.

"I'm hungry," she said.

"So am I."

We found a Chinese restaurant, tucked between an all-hour drycleaner and an outlet store, where we ordered everything on the menu and ate like it was our last meal.

After I realized that our relationship was in trou-ble, I begged Veronica to go back there with me.

"We had fun last time, didn't we?"

"Yes, but—"

"Then we'll do it again. We'll have fun again."

"You're mad if you think the world works that way."

After a while though, I wore her down and she agreed to go back. It almost worked, but when you try to go back to where a memory occurred for the sake of reliving that memory, you're always disappointed. Some-times, you're better off never going back.

———

IN 1968, MY UNCLE LEFT the firehouse and was deployed in Vietnam, where he served as a runner in combat. His football skills were once again useful, so I imagine he was quite happy out there. Happiness, however, is fickle and fleeting. Three weeks into the tour he returned with a finger missing and a gimp that made him look like a lame rabbit when he walked. An honorable discharge and a Purple Heart were his rewards.

He paid a steep price for it though. He would never run again. Never again do what he loved. And whenever geese would fly overhead he would point to the sky with his short, bony fingers and shout: "Take cover! Raid! Take cover!"

There were many times when I found him on the front porch, preaching the same tired stories about combat to whoever he could get to listen. Sometimes, I think that given the choice, he would have made the trade voluntarily. A ring finger in exchange for one of the highest honors the country can bestow, along with a lifetime of storytelling and an undeserved sense of entitlement to everything that wasn't his.

That day, when he was getting on me for scaring Kaylee away, was the day I decided to stop being a push over. I swore I'd live for myself and not be concerned with what other people thought of me. It was liberating— no longer seeking the approval of teachers, friends, and strangers—letting myself go.

The man was never capable of love, but losing that finger sealed the deal. He displayed the Purple Heart in a box nailed to the wall in his bedroom so that it would be the first thing he saw in the morning and the last thing he saw at night—until the day I stole it while he was out of the house and threw it into a pond because that was as close to hell as I could get the thing.

"Where is it?" he yelled.

"Where's what?"

"Don't play dumb, boy. I know it was you!"

"I don't know what you mean. Going senile, finally, or what?"

"My heart is gone!"

"No shit."

"My heart is gone, you little fuck up!"

"I already know that you have no heart, old man."

"Did you know that you were an accident?"

NOBODY LIKES DRIVING in front of a hearse. I swear to God it's one of the creepiest fucking things.

Veronica got a kick out of it though.

"Come on. That's funny," she said. "Death in the rearview mirror."

I couldn't tell which way she was looking at it. Had we moved past death or had it always been there, lurking?

She put her hand between my legs and I tried not to swerve. She unzipped my jeans and it was as if she was trying to tempt fate.

"You'd better stop before we get into an accident," I told her.

But there was no stopping her.

She finished me off, and we didn't crash. From her purse, she pulled a pack of gum and began chewing. At the next stoplight, the hearse made a left and we made a right. That's when she turned to me with gravity pooling her eyes, and said, "There are no such things as accidents, Matt. Everything that's meant to happen, happens."

IT HAPPENED ON A STORMY Monday evening in September.

I was a ten-year-old boy in the sixth grade, and middle school was still new.

My uncle and I were on our way to a Yankee game that would never be played. Weather reports and Major League Baseball history will tell different versions of this same story.

My father was bowling. Doing the same thing he did every Monday night with the guys from his department.

I was excited because it was considered cool if you went to school the next day and told your friends that you had been to Yankee Stadium the night before.

"I knew this was a bad idea," my uncle grumbled.

There was a massive amount of traffic on I-95, even before the rain started. For an hour we sat on the George Washington Bridge, suspended above the Hudson River in his small '98 Maxima, and I imagined the bridge collapsing—all the people in their cars hovering in the brief stillness before the decent and unavoidable crash.

"I need to take piss," my uncle said.

And with that he gulped down what was left of his water bottle, leaned over my lap to open the glove box, and pulled out a pocket knife.

"Open it," he said. "Cut the plastic all the way around."

After a few minutes of struggling, I was able to rip the top of the water bottle away. My uncle took the bottle from me, pulled his dick out the leg of his shorts, and started urinating into it.

"If I was you, I wouldn't need to make a bigger opening," he said, still peeing.

When he was done, he opened the car door and poured the piss out onto the bridge.

"Put this on the floor by your leg," he said, handing me the empty bottle, "Just in case I need it again."

When we finally got across the bridge, the storm was at its worst. Our tickets were down the third-baseline, under the mezzanine. Somehow, our seats were still dry. We had been sitting in them no more than ten minutes when the voice of legendary announcer Bob Sheppard rang out as loud as the thunder.

Ladies and gentlemen, tonight's game has been cancelled due to inclement weather. You will be able to re-use your tickets to attend a game at a later date, to be announced. Thank you, and please get home safely.

The traffic for the bathroom was as bad as the traffic had been on the bridge, but my uncle insisted on going before we left the stadium. Walking into the men's room with him, I remember seeing all the ticket stubs discarded like rubble across the wet floor.

I remember flying back across the bridge, the road ahead as clear as the nights to follow would be long.

And I remember wondering the next day how many people I may have seen the night before in that stadium bathroom that must have died the next morning when the towers fell—exactly as they were meant to fall.

SHE BROKE UP WITH ME on a Tuesday.

"You're improvising again," Veronica said. "It's cute for a while, but it gets old."

Improvising. Instead of desperate or pathetic.

This is why I needed her. She was so gentle.

Compassionate still, even though I wasn't getting it.

"You want to know why I've let this go on as long as I have? Because I know you're a good guy, Matt."

"Why don't we go to Vegas? We can even stay there. Gamble on me...please."

Just then, her roommate came back from class, took one look at me, and rolled her eyes. "Can't you take the fucking hint?"

"Rachel, don't," Veronica said.

I was out of there faster than my uncle at a bar when a hippie walked in.

In the middle of campus there was a pond with willow trees and benches around it. When I was sad, I used to sit there and people-watch as kids came and went around the macadam that circled the water.

She caught up to me while I was throwing rocks. Took a seat on my right and stared at the people going around in circles.

"Matt, you're so...I know you mean well, but you're so...misguided."

I turned my head and winced. She didn't have to see my face to know that she had wounded me.

She put a cold hand on my arm. "That was wrong of me. Maybe I'm not any good at this either."

"Veronica, if you want to leave me, just leave me. I'm done trying to hold onto you."

We are all moving in circles, each of us lost in our own way.

The trick to tossing rocks is all in the arc. It's not just the force of the throw or the sound of the splash, it's watching it float. Up in a moment, down in the next.

Like everything.

Hovering in that brief stillness.

Before the descent and unavoidable crash.

"Quit that or you'll scare the fish away," she scolded.

"There aren't any fish in this water. It's too polluted."

"Well, then in that case…" She picked up a rock and threw it. It fell short in the tall grass by the edge of the pond and she made a disappointed face.

So I grabbed another piece of gravel from the ground, covered her hand with mine, and said: "Like this."

Together we threw pebbles and broken sticks, cursing life.

Each impact rippling through the surface of the water like tree rings. Passionate echoes of one central point that inevitably faded away.

Geese Love the Rain

"THE WORLD IS ENDING," Scuzzy told me.

"When?"

"Right now."

"Are you sure?"

"Yeah, man."

"How can you be sure?" I asked.

"From the fallout."

"Nuclear fallout?"

"Yeah, man. Look at this stuff. It's everywhere." He lifted a shovel of snow to my face. He was clearing the walkway to the front steps of his apartment.

"Too late for us, man, so they make us handle it because we're already goners."

"Who's they?"

"The government. Corrupt as shit." Scuzzy was always talking about the government. He had a conspiracy theory for everything. While we were talking, I noticed the way his left foot twitched.

"Do you have anymore?" I asked him.

"No. I snorted it all before you came over."

He was lying, but he thought he was telling the truth.

"You know, I'll bet this stuff probably tastes pretty good." I lifted a handful of snow to my face.

"No, man. No. Don't." He reached out his hand, begging me to stop. "Please don't, man."

I stuck my tongue into it, licked some up, and watched him as the snow melted in my mouth.

"Oh no. No, man. You can't eat this stuff, man. It'll make your symptoms worse. You'll start growing another leg, another eye, or some shit."

I cupped my hands together, made a snowball, and threw it at him. Direct hit, right in the face.

"No! Fuck me! I'm fucked!" He dropped to his knees, screaming, writhing around in the imaginary fallout with real terror, real grief.

Scuzzy had long, greasy, light-brown hair, thin eyebrows that ran too far down past the sides of his eyes, and a wide jaw that made his scrawny shoulders look stronger. He was a friend of mine with a habit of being in the wrong place at the right time.

"My name is William S. Cuzzy," he said to me the first time we met. "But everyone just calls me Scuzzy."

Scuzzy had been pulling out of a McDonalds drive thru when a little girl ran out into the parking lot right in front of his car. The kid was alright, but they took her to the hospital in an ambulance as a precaution. Scuzzy was so shaken up by it that he practically told me his whole life story when he saw me standing there, watching.

"I didn't see her, man. It wasn't my fault, was it? Do you think it was my fault? Man, I hope they don't. I wasn't going fast or being reckless. I'm not a violent person, man. Really. I was born in California."

As if that explained something.

"We moved here when I was young, man. My mother is a waitress and my father was a cardiologist before a malpractice suit turned him into someone more like me. When I was twelve, my sister, my brother, and me would fight over his blank prescription pad. Between our yelling over it and his wild punishments because of the yelling, there was never any quiet time around our house. That's probably why we never saw mom much, man. She used to take doubles down at the restaurant even though dad pulled in six figures."

He paused to breathe, shook his head, and turned to spit before continuing.

"She just wanted to be away from the house while all of us were there, so she would work all night, come home and sleep all day, at least until we moved out. Now, she's much happier. I dunno when, but my brother, sister, and me realized that if we worked together it was much easier to get the pad away from dad without him noticing. Man, we'd all just split the pills we got from it. I studied dad's scribbled signature—I'm very good at things like that."

After he picked himself off the ground, I lifted another snowball, got ready to pelt him again.

"Why do geese love the rain?" Scuzzy asked, moving on from his concern about the fallout, forgetting that the world was ending.

"I don't know why, but I have a feeling that you're going to tell me."

"No, I was asking you, man."

"Oh, well then, they love the rain because it feels good."

"I thought you didn't know why geese love the rain," he said.

"I didn't when you first asked, but now it seems pretty obvious."

"They like it 'cause it feels good…" he mulled.

"Yes, they don't care how they look. They just do it because it feels good."

"We could all stand to be a little more like geese," he said, spitting in the snow.

Scuzzy sat down cross-legged on the shoveled concrete walkway, his foot still twitching. There were piles of salt in the middle of the street in front of his apartment. Slush had built up on the curb by the sidewalk. A few kids were laughing and pointing at a friend that had stepped into the dirty sludge. Poor guy's pant leg was soaked up the knee.

"Do you have anymore? I know you do, Scuzz. Don't bullshit me."

"Haha, you see that kid? Geese, fucking geese, man. They love the fucking rain, those geese."

"I know you have more. I want some."

"I'm feeling like a goose. You wanna feel like a goose too? Follow me."

Scuzzy jolted up, ran to the front steps, slipping on the ice as he went inside. I followed him, picked up the shovel he'd left behind. If something is left outside around campus, it's going to get stolen, no matter what it is. People are greedy like that.

Inside, I found him sitting on a metal foldout chair at the kitchen table, chopping like a mad man with a razor blade, using a credit card to manipulate a pile of white powder into two straight lines.

"You want some, Mr. Goose? You got it."

"Where did you get that card?" Scuzzy didn't have credit.

"Found it, man," he said, lowering his nose.

I did the line he'd laid out for me. "That's doubtful."

"Really found it, man. It was on the floor somewhere, so I picked it up."

I held a stare at him until he crumbled. "Alright, I stole it," he said, wiping snot away from his nose. "But the man was lying on his stomach on a bench in the park, so his wallet was really close to the ground."

I smiled, plucked the card from his hand like a mother would as she takes something forbidden away from her child, took a scissor to it before throwing it in the trash.

FEELING GOOD, WE LEFT his apartment looking to bother people. It was getting nasty outside. The cold bit our noses as the air hissed around us. I turned toward Scuzzy and found him holding what looked like tiny sticks of dynamite between his fingers.

"What are those things?" I asked.

"Firecrackers. You hungry for some?" He twirled them around in his hands, looked down at them with care.

"Nah, I never saw the fun in blowing stuff up," I answered.

"Never saw the fun? Follow me."

In nothing but a t-shirt, ripped jeans, and sneakers, Scuzzy took off through the wind with a hiss of his own, laughing out loud and yelling, "Get the fuck out of my way!" to cars that almost hit him in the street.

Somehow, with everything that was going on, I remembered to zip up my hoodie and put gloves on. I followed Scuzzy into a classroom building, taking the seat next to him in the back corner of a large lecture hall.

The professor at the front of the room could only be described as a cartoon character. He was a tall, lanky, middle-aged man with bushy grey hair that pushed out and hung down past his shoulders. He reminded me of Emmett "Doc" Brown from *Back to the Future* and Otto Mann from *The Simpsons*. I had heard about him from one of my friends who'd taken his Philosophy class. His name was Michael Beyton.

"He works for NASA," my friend had told me. "The guy seems crazy, but apparently he's a fucking genius."

His hair bounced when he talked.

"Life is a party! Enjoy yourself every day! That is the key to happiness, my friends. We can all teach one another. In fact—YOU be MY professor! The important thing is knowing that you will all be a GREAT success!"

It was a room full of smiles. Professor Beyton was waving a laser pointer at his PowerPoint presentation, foreshadowing the key points of a lecture he would never get to give.

"When you hear the birds outside, they're having a party! They don't care about stoo-pid civil-i-zation. When a bird wants to leave, he doesn't worry about a mortgage or taxes, he just has a party! If it wasn't winter, we could hear them out there, having a party while we're in here thanks to stoo-pid civil-i-zation."

The hall resembled a movie theatre's layout: a center aisle, bisecting the long rows of seats, with exit aisles on either side. There were two-hundred students in the class. Most had shed their jackets and stripped down to their t-shirts because The University pumped thick, heavy heat into each building.

Someone's cellphone went off and Beyton stopped mid-sentence, smiled, bobbed his head. "Thank you! Thank you for the party!"

Without saying a word, Scuzzy handed me a firecracker. We each pulled lighters out of our pockets and held the low grade explosives to the ground. We leaned forward in our chairs to light them and one loud bang ensued.

People began running, dozens and dozens of students falling over one another to get to the exits. Kids were moving their lips, screaming, but not making any noise. I was amazed that so many people could panic without making a sound. Then I turned to Scuzzy and saw his mouth moving—his voice was distant, as though he was talking under water—and it became clear that people were making noise that I couldn't hear. My ears were ringing like a shell-shocked soldier's.

Scuzzy held up his hands, blood running down his fingers, down his forearms, to the points of his elbows, where it dripped to the floor. He began talking to himself. Counting to ten—an inventory of his fingers. I raised my own hands, touched the unblemished skin through the patches of my gloves that had been blown away. That's when I saw that I was still holding my firecracker. The damn thing had never gone off. It was a failure that brought unexpected sadness, something so simple that I had not gotten right. Scuzzy dropped to a knee and it occurred to me that not everybody was running. Many students were on the floor between the rows of seats, taking cover, with their arms wrapped around their heads. Before either of us could do anything else, we were pushed by our terrified peers into the crowd along the side aisle, swept away like twigs caught in a river's current.

Scuzzy put his hands in his pockets. I removed my hoodie, dropped it on the floor, and exited like everyone else, with goose-bumped arms. Keeping our heads down, we walked as far as the panic would take us until the crowd dispersed, at which point both of us took off running back to Scuzzy's apartment. We barely made it inside the front door before we collapsed on the floor, belly-laughing so hard neither of us made a sound.

Soon, our hearing returned.

"My fucking hands," he said holding them up. "They burn like piss. Your face, your face is bleeding, man."

I went to the bathroom to look in the mirror. My scar had opened up.

"It does this sometimes," I said to Scuzzy, walking back into the kitchen with a wad of toilet paper to my cheek.

"They're gonna catch us, man. There's no way they won't catch us."

All happiness was gone from his face. He looked like he had when he told me the world was ending.

"Probably," I said.

"What the fuck do we do, man? What the fuck?"

"Just wait. Maybe the cameras didn't see us walk in. Anybody in that room could have set the shit off. We walked in like five minutes after the class started. We were just late to class, dude. People are late every day."

"Yeah, yeah. Kids walk in late all the time."

Scuzzy walked to the sink and ran his hands under cold water. With his fingers still dripping wet, he went to the refrigerator, opened the freezer, and pulled out a bottle of vodka. It was strange that he didn't scream when he poured it on his wounds. It should have stung, but Scuzzy didn't let on if it hurt. He poured the vodka up and down his forearms, over the track marks, too. I remembered being there for some of them, looked down at the marks on my own arms and wondered if vodka would sting them. Taking out his lighter again, Scuzzy began to cauterize the bleeding areas of his fingers.

"I'm not going to the hospital, man. I'm not going to the hospital. Corrupt as shit, those hospitals. All them greedy doctors just trying to get at your wallet. Man, oh man, the bastards. Did you know those cameras in the hospital are just for show? Like there's no actual film or digital recording in there, man. That's what they do to try to get you to behave, to behave like they want you to behave. And most people do, the cattle. You don't think the doctors know that, man? They know there's no live camera in those black circle things. They stick their middle fingers up at those cameras on the ceiling. They can do whatever the fuck they want to you while you're in their care and get away with it, the bastards."

He repeated different variations of the same rant a half-dozen times.

My knee was shaking up and down like crazy. I began watching it as if it would tell me something. I counted how many times it bounced up and down as we waited for someone to come for us. We stayed inside as everyone else poked their heads outside to see what all the sirens were screeching for. We refused to answer the texts asking if we'd heard about the possible shooting at The University...ignored the Tweets, too. We waited until the sky turned dark and made the police lights down the street visible from a mile off. We waited for days after, certain that we would be caught, but no one ever came.

No one ever comes.

Lost Kittens

FRESHMAN YEAR MY BUDDY Sash and I used to chase deer around campus when we were bored and feeling alone. The first time he saw one, we were playing drunk Mario Kart on Nintendo64.

"Fuck you, fucking Peach!" He'd fallen off the road, thrown the controller into the painted cinderblock wall that separated his room from mine in the basement of freshman House 24.

"You owe me another controller," I said. It was the second one he'd broken on me in as many races. "What the hell am I supposed to do when Skeeter comes over looking to drink and drive later and I only have one controller?"

Sash spit on the wall, he loved video games and hated to lose them.

"The fuck is that?" he asked.

"Gravity," I said. His brown spit headed for the floor, got caught in a cement crease that separated two bricks, and stopped just long enough for me to look away. "Oh, that's a deer."

"No shit it's a deer. I know what it is. I've just never seen one. We don't have those in Dubai."

Outside my window, a small buck stood eating acorns off the ground beneath an oak tree. It was beautiful, antlers wrapped in velvet, fur goldened by the setting sun. As Sash looked out at the deer I knew that this would become one of his things, like throwing cupcakes at the side of House 23.

"Be right back," he said. He left the room and went next door. I began picking up the pieces of the broken controllers when I heard a noise. The deer shot across the street, almost got railroaded by a neon-blue Hyundai.

I walked into Sash's room and found him standing in front of an open window with a Nerf gun in his hand.

"The hunt is on," he said.

Like a bullet, he took off running, hit the stairs, taking them two at a time. I followed, dodging left and right to avoid his boney elbows they swung. When we got to the top of the fourth floor, I popped the screen off the window in the floor lounge, and we climbed the metal rungs on the wall outside up to the roof.

As he ran toward the edge I pictured him tripping, falling like a broken controller, gravity pulling him down like the brown spit on my wall. When he got to the edge, he aimed the gun, pulled the trigger, and shot.

"Fucking missed," he said.

"It's because you pulled the trigger too hard," I said. "Don't jerk it, breathe while you squeeze it. It should surprise you when the gun goes off."

He looked at me funny, as if he was seeing me for the first time. "You stopped messaging me when I said I was from Dubai."

Below, the deer grazed its way into the woods, unaware that it had just been shot at. I had no idea what Sash was talking about.

"Back in August," he said. "We were talking in the House 24 group chat on Facebook. We DM'ed when we learned we'd be neighbors. When I told you where I was from, you shut up. Probably thought I was some terrorist."

Adrenaline made my blood feel cold. How do you recover from something as damaging as that?

I was saved by what happened next. A car passed and ran over something small. If we hadn't seen it, the cracking sound would have been mistaken for a crushed soda can.

We both said "Shit" at the same time.

"I saw it, too," Sash said before I could get another word out.

I put my hand on my forehead and tried not to vomit. Failed. Then apologized to Sash.

"I've seen worse," he said. "Pull your shit together, we better get down there."

We both knew what we were looking for, but I was unsure I wanted to find it.

"Maybe we should let the coyotes have it," I said.

"Boom! Found it."

Sash stood over the pancaked kitten and looked sad for the first time since I'd known him.

"It's eyes were green," he said. "I have green eyes. That could have been me."

THE RAIN CAME BEFORE the blackout, as rain often does. My phone and laptop were both dead, plugged into a wall that refused to give power. I laid on my bed with my hand down my pants waiting for something to happen.

I reached for the bottle of Mederma next to my bed, and rubbed some on my face. The door was open and Sash walked in.

"Boom!" he said, shooting me with a Nerf gun and laughing. "War is upon us, my friend."

"Huh?"

"We of House 24 have come under attack by insurgents of the wretched House 23."

He handed me a loaded gun, laughed louder.

"What's so funny?" I asked him.

"What's so funny, bahahaha. That's good, but war, son. War is upon us. There are a dozen enemies,

enemies of the Republic raiding the rooms of our beloved House 24 as we speak."

"I want some before we go out."

"Ask and you shall receive. The gas always makes war more pleasant, more fun."

"It also makes it easier to die!" I said.

This brought a big smile to his face. He put his arm over my shoulder and walked me to his room. The kid loved to share life with people. But I was the only one he shared tanks of nitrous oxide with.

We were sitting in his open closet, giggling to ourselves, when Skeeter walked in wearing a headband with Nerf darts arranged in it like a bandoleer.

"Let's go, ladies. We've pushed them back. Now we're chasing after them to raid House 23. Gotta show 'em who's boss. Make sure they know what'll happen if they come after us again!"

"Raid!"

Sash loved raids. Before either of us could stop laughing at Skeeter's headband, the three of us were running across the small lawn that connected the two buildings, shooting invisible airplanes out of the sky as they tried to bomb us from overhead. We got inside by taking a hostage and forcing him to open the dorm building with his student ID because each ID only worked for the dorm that you lived in.

"Spread out. Knock on every door. Shoot everyone you can. No one escapes without a Nerf dart in the belly!" Sash yelled as Skeeter and I ran up the stairs behind him.

"I'll take the first floor. Sash, you take the second floor. Matt, you take the third floor." Skeeter pointed and we separated.

No one answered the first few doors I knocked on. But the third door opened to a girl drying her blue hair with a bath towel. Her big brown eyes turned yellow in the hall light.

"Please, tell me your name before you shoot me?" she asked, dropping the towel to the floor and putting her hands up.

"Matthew, Matthew Rose."

"I'm Francesca. You boys playing Nerf wars again?"

I wanted to tell her right there how real she was.

"There's no time. They'll be up here soon. We need to move fast."

I grabbed her by the arm and she followed me to the stairs. We kept close to the wall—close to each other—trying to avoid Sash, Skeeter, and anyone else who had invaded from House 24. I led her down, and when we got outside, she grabbed my hand and we took off running. The wind blew and a mixture of nail polish and aerosol intoxicated me.

From behind Sash yelled, "Mutiny! The bastard! Skeeter, mutiny!"

The rain soaked our clothes. Our socks squished in puddles as we splashed toward the highway beyond the dining hall. In the field behind Skillet, there were a dozen shirtless boys covered in mud, playing football in the storm. They looked slippery, muscles shining. Some of them were limping. Without caution, we crossed the highway and learned that it is impossible to sprint through a cemetery unless it's something you've done before. Headstone after headstone got in our way as we split apart to navigate them. I threw glances over both shoulders, not to see if anyone chased us, but hoping to catch glimpses of ghosts that may have gazed on at us— startled, envious of life.

We stopped beneath the overhang of a mausoleum, sat down with our backs against holy concrete, laughing with honesty that had eluded me and Sash.

"You have a beautiful name, Matthew Rose," she said, ringing her hair.

I half-expected her hands to turn blue.

"You know that treason is punishable by death?" I asked.

"I'm honored that you would risk your life for me."

I reached for her hand again, but she pulled it away. She stood up, and began running back through the cemetery the way we'd come with much more grace than either of us had a moment ago. While I chased her, I noticed piles of weeds that had been left in the middle of a sidewalk next to a garden. They lay dying there, browning at the edges, decomposing faster in the rain than they would have in the sun.

That's when I saw the second kitten. Neck broken, just as dead as the one from the night before.

I looked back ahead for Francesca but she was gone. For a second, I questioned whether or not she was even real. A pale leg darted out from behind a headstone and tripped me. I hit the dirt hard, almost cracked my skull on the next row of stones and missed the swift kiss of irony by inches.

"All's fair in war," she said before taking off so that I could chase her again.

She was fast and I didn't think I would ever catch her. But hours later I woke up to the blinking clock of my micro-fridge and found her next to me. Blue hair disheveled, face distorted by a dream.

"I'VE GOT SOMETHING MARVELOUS to show you," Sash said to me. "While you were off playboying yesterday, Skeeter and I went on an expedition."

"An expedition?"

"Boom! That's right. But I've got to show it to you. It's more marvelous to see it than to hear about it."

He pulled out a small pipe, sparked a lighter, and smoked his hashish the way he did every hour on the hour.

"You see that trail into the woods right there?" he pointed out his window.

I nodded.

"Come with me," he said.

The ground was muddy. Each step triggered the smell of earth. Above we heard birds cawing and through the branches and brand new leaves I saw them circling.

"Vultures," I pointed.

"It's just a little further," Sash said. "A little further, Matty boy, and you shall see a marvel."

The trail led into a small oval-shaped clearing in the woods, and there it was.

"Boom!" Sash crossed his arms. He spit into a puddle and the splash echoed like a raindrop from the past. "Do you see how it just vanishes?"

Before us both, was twenty feet of rusted train track, spiked into the ground, an end without a destination on either side. At once, I felt a buzz all around us. Ghost-workers carrying steel, hammering it into the dirt.

"What do you think it means?" Sash asked me.

"Life," I answered.

I told him about the second kitten I'd seen yesterday at the cemetery. He kicked one of the rails with his foot. The vibrations lifted birds in nearby trees to flight.

Brought me back to the vultures circling, and I began walking toward them.

"The fuck you going? Wait up, Matty boy."

I smelt it before I saw it. Got my nose under the front collar of my shirt before inhaling gnats.

Sash vomited, apologized, and said, "I've still seen worse."

I thought of how beautiful it had been a few days ago, antlers wrapped in velvet, eating acorns beneath the tree outside my window. How full of life it had been as it darted across the street and just missed the Hyundai.

"Maybe your shot was more accurate than we thought," I said.

Sash gave me a big grin then, pulled his pipe back out and lit it. "Or maybe it got hit by a fucking train."

"I DIDN'T GET HER NUMBER," I told Skeeter. "If it's meant to be, she knows where to find me and I know where to find her."

We were walking toward Nightclub, on our way to forget about everything.

"Just seems like a waste," he said.

If he only knew what real waste was.

"Did I ever tell you my rape story?" he asked me.

"You serious?"

He turned toward me, but kept his feet moving. "Dead serious."

He pulled out a pocket flask, shook it, found it empty, and put it back in his pocket.

"You know that girl Rachel from upstairs in the house?"

"Yeah," I said. "The big girl with the blonde hair and flat face?"

"Yeah, that bitch."

"You're kidding me."

"I already told you I'm dead serious. Just before winter break I was coming back to House 24 after a frat party out on Main Street. I'm totally drunk off my ass stumbling through the hall, when Rachel sees me and makes it her business to escort me back to my room. Next thing I know, I'm waking up in bed with her."

"Shit."

"Hold on, it gets better. So I wake up and I'm flipping out. All of a sudden, she starts laughing at me saying, 'You couldn't even get it up. You couldn't even keep your dick hard.' I'm like, 'Get the fuck out. Get out of my room.' Then she goes around telling everyone that I slept with her and I couldn't keep my dick up. Not that anyone could around her sober, but I was fucked up out of my mind."

"You should tell someone," I said, and as soon as the words left my mouth I felt like a dumbass. Who was there to tell? Who would care?

I'd never seen Skeeter embarrassed before, and I felt touched. There were a thousand fucked up stories I could tell him, but sometimes when someone tells you something that they've been keeping inside for a long time, the last thing they want is for you to try to relate to them. To change the subject away from what he'd just shared, with an anecdote from my own past would have been a cruel, common mistake.

"Anyway," he said, "you think Sash is here?"

We'd gotten to Nightclub. It was just before nine-thirty and the line was already out the door. Skeeter took out his fake ID and headed for the crowd of people. I grabbed his arm, pulled him toward the front door, and flashed my VIP card at the bouncer.

"How the fuck did you get one of those?"

"I have two of them actually." I took another one out, handed it to Skeeter, and he looked at me like I'd given him what he'd asked for for Christmas. "Sash gave one to me because he's like their number one customer here. If I had to guess I'd say he's in there now, toward the back wall, buying rounds of shots for everyone he knows. The other one I got when one of the bartenders figured out I have money to spend. They just want your money. That's all everyone ever wants."

Inside, we found Sash standing on his tiptoes, counting heads with his fingers.

"Seventeen," he mouthed to the bartender. She dropped what she was doing to take Sash's order and the guy she hadn't finished serving yet shot her dirty looks. Sash saw Skeeter and me and said, "Make it nineteen."

"You're a good man, Dubian," I said.

"And you're about to be a drunk man, Rosanne. Boom! See what I did there?"

Sash passed out shots to everyone he had counted, receiving his "Thank yous" with grace, as any good mayor should. A moment later, he leaned in close to my ear and whispered, "You look tense, Matty boy. You look so tense that you're slow. I want to make you go fast. Do you wanna go fast, buddy?"

"I'm not smoking that hash with you again."

"I'm not talking about the hash. I'm talking about having sex with you. And by having sex with you, I'm talking about fucking your mind."

"You're out of your mind, Dubian."

"No, I already came inside yours. Boom!"

Without warning he stabbed a needle into my upper thigh, right through my jeans, turned his body so that it shielded the syringe from prying eye, and pressed a clear liquid into me.

"Mind successfully fucked," he said. "Matty, my boy, you're about to go pretty fucking fast!"

My eyes widened. I looked at him with an *are you fucking kidding me?* look, and he stuck his pink tongue out at me.

"Vroom, vroom! We got a whizz kid here!"

This cracked him up, so much so that he had to rest his head on the bar.

Ear-blinded by the music, it looked like he was crying. The bartender rushed over to him, put an attentive hand on his shoulder, and looked relieved when she saw that he was laughing. He said something to her and she went straight to pouring bottles of Evian water into glasses of ice.

"You're gonna need it. Boy, are you gonna need the water. You're about to go so fast, Matty kid, buddy."

He was euphoric. So happy with life it was inspiring.

Skeeter had made his way over to the center of the crowd where guys and girls were doing body shots off two girls lying flat on a wooden table.

I spent the next few hours dancing without shame. So lost that for a little while I didn't care if I would ever be found.

Then the lights came on and the bouncers started clearing everyone out of Nightclub.

"What the fuck?" Sash held his arms up and out wide like Jesus addressing a crowd. He looked so beautiful in the blue barlights.

I grabbed one more water bottle from the bartender and went for the door. Outside, a crowd was forming around two EMTs that were tending to an Asian man who was passed out on his back.

"He's going into cardiac arrest," one of the men working on him yelled. Sash and I pushed our way to the front of the circle in time to see the first shocks from the defibrillator.

"Rip his shirt all the way off. That's it."

"Clear!"

The man's limbs jerked toward the sky. He looked like he was in his mid-twenties—probably a grad student—but he may have been older. Thin bangs hung low on his face, wisps of hair that I pictured lasting many years in a coffin.

"Clear!"

Through the shocked silence came the faint sound of glass breaking. The man's watch struck the concrete sidewalk, and I took it as a sign that his time was up. His other arm fell so that his hand rested across his chest, a corpse with one foot already in the grave.

My heart was beating out of my chest. I tried to wish some of its energy into the dying man.

"Don't look so paranoid," Sash whispered in my ear. "Adrenaline, my friend. That's what we all want. That's what the heart needs."

I looked back just in time to see the paramedic lift a syringe above his head and plunge it into the man's chest. All at once, the peace vanished from his face and it flooded again with the pain of life.

"Let's head over to Tony's Pizzeria," Skeeter suggested, but Sash and I weren't hungry.

"Let them overcharge the other drunkards," Sash said.

"I'll catch up with you ladies later, then," Skeeter said, joining the stream of kids heading from Nightclub to Tony's.

I looked at Sash just as his eyes shot open wide.

"What now?" I asked him.

"Matty, boy, turn around and tell me if you see it, too."

Behind me, on a streetlamp, was a poster. We got closer and I read it aloud: "Missing, litter of three kittens. Reward for safe return. If found please call…"

"Shitfuck," Sash said.

Same lime-green eyes. Same color fur. I thought right away of a little girl sitting at home waiting for a phone call.

"We should tell them what happened," I said.

"What's the number?" Sash pulled out his phone, dropped it. It cracked like the dying man's watch on the sidewalk.

"Still don't believe in phone cases?"

"Shut up and give me your phone," he said.

"No. We can't call. A phone call would be too cruel. It would give the little girl hope."

"It could be a little boy," Sash said. "No reason it can't be a little boy."

He kicked his phone into the gutter. *Do you see how it just vanishes?* It splashed when it hit the bottom of the drain and made me think of the third kitten.

"I'm going after it," I told him.

"You stopped talking to me after I told you I was from Dubai," Sash said.

It knocked the wind out of me a little more the second time, when I realized that it wasn't going to go away and that there was nothing I could ever do to take back my mistake. No matter how close we were, this would always divide us.

"I love you, anyway," he told me, punching my shoulder. "Let's find that last kitten."

I pictured us as heroes. Returning pieces of faith to a child who had learned too soon that life is more pain than joy.

"Can you imagine if we really found it?" Sash asked as we walked toward the freshmen houses. "Boom! What a story that would make."

"We're going to find it."

"No vultures." He pointed toward the dark sky and I noticed the stars. Shattered parts of something that would never be whole again.

"Oh, my. What do we have here?" Sash froze in his tracks.

A deer stood in the middle of a dorm courtyard.

"Don't. You're never going to catch it," I said.

"And you're never going to find that lost kitten, either. But you're sure as hell going to try. Boom!" And then he took off running.

Putting one slim leg in front of the other, his curly hair bounced with every step, and for a second I thought that he might catch it. They both disappeared into the night like the present into the past. Unstatic, wild, and free. Someday, when I am too old to chase deer, too old to run through a cemetery…when memories of what life was once like are all that I have left, this is how I will remember him.

Tomorrow is Monday

M ONDAY

Mondays matter to everyone in the world except for those in college. Days blur together like tears, they leave your eyes fogged and you daydreaming life away.

You start the week by forcing yourself to get out of bed. You wet your hands and run a comb through your hair. There is an early bus to catch across campus for your first class, a lecture hall where everyone will be just like you; tired, grumpy, and helpless. On your way, through the dorm building, you stop at a water fountain and slosh cold water around in your mouth to get rid of the morning breath because you didn't have time to brush your teeth. There is a strong coffee smell in the water fountain. You are up early, but someone else woke up earlier. A subtle reminder that you are never the best, there is always someone better than you whether you choose to acknowledge it or not.

The grass outside is beautiful—a little too beautiful. In fact, it isn't even grass at all. Graduation is approaching soon for some poor souls, and The University is rolling out grass carpets between the sidewalk and street all over campus. It is important for them to keep up appearances—to create the desired illusion of care. Soon, parents and grandparents will be coming, holding the hands of your little brothers and sisters, who will bend down to touch the grass that is greener than any grass they have seen in their lives.

Oh, what lovely grass, your grandma will say.

The campus really is beautiful, your mother will agree.

The University knows what it's doing. While on the bus, you notice the flowers that have been planted beneath every tree and you wish that the campus always looked this new.

You feel awake. A fleeting moment where you've been able to shake the fog from your eyes and realize your breath. Not even class can dampen this wonderful mood.

When class is over, you walk toward Passion Pond and see a girl in rain boots feeding chocolate chip cookies to the ducks. They are cute as hell and they've got her surrounded, cornered her against a tree. She kneels down, petting them while they eat. Nearby, sticking out of the bushes, there is a metal abstract art sculpture that looks down on picnic tables where someone is playing the guitar.

It's easy being at college because all you have to do is take care of yourself. The only mood that matters to you is your own. When you live at home, during the summers, you're with other people and you have to care about their moods, their feelings. You eat when they want to eat and lock yourself in your room at a reasonable hour because you don't want to keep anybody up.

Back at your dorm you take two bites out of an apple before leaving on the windowsill overlooking a large sidewalk where other students rush to class, each person on his or her unique schedule. There are a few hours before your next class and you decide to take a shower in the middle of the day because you can. It's fun to think of all the people in their office buildings, at work, while you're naked in the shower.

It's raining after your last class. A group of kids huddle beneath an umbrella at a picnic table, smoking hookah. The rain beats down hard, wetting the new grass around them, but pressed shoulder to shoulder they are safe. There is a special camaraderie they share—each passing the hose to the left—something so simple in the way they are all together. You realize that the moment is special.

It's time to feed yourself dinner. The takeout line is short at the dining hall, but the wind blows hard enough at the automatic door to slide it open. You start to shiver because you're wearing shorts. A nice boy with a young face tries to pull the door shut against its will.

"I wonder if there's any way to keep the rain out," he says.

"It's okay. I'll be fine."

He smiles, unaware that people don't go out of their way to help one another anymore. "I'll try to block the wind for you."

"What's your name?" you ask.

"Billy," he says, unzipping his hoodie, spreading his arms out wide.

You notice his rosy cheeks and wonder if they are that way because of the storm or because that's the way they are.

"Yours?" he asks.

You're embarrassed that you forgot to say your own name back. His personality is captivating. He seems aware of this. A lot of people must forget to tell him their names. After you tell him yours, he says, "Niceta meetya" and seems to mean it.

With your food in a plastic bag and a soft drink in your hand, you leave the takeout wing of the dining hall.

The rain is now a light mist falling from a cloudless sky. It's as if you are trapped in the thinnest of clouds. All the buildings always look so clean after it storms.

TUESDAY

There's a reason why you keep your hair long. If you sit in the back of the lecture hall, you can run the headphone wires of your iPod up the inside of your shirt and your hair will hide the ear buds. You wouldn't even bother showing up, but this is one of those teachers that doesn't believe in putting her PowerPoints online, so if you want the notes you will have to wake up and drag yourself to class. She's a young teacher, very attractive, not far removed from being a student herself. If she's wise to your ways she hasn't said anything. You wish you could split note-duty with a friend so you'd only have to be here half the time, but you don't have any friends in this class.

In the back row of the lecture hall, to your right, there is a boy sitting alone, groping himself through his jeans, thinking nobody is watching. Someone has brought a laser pointer to class and is making circles with it on one of the sidewalls. Only a few people notice it. Whoever is holding it is trying to spell something, but their hand is unsteady.

Outside are the lunch trucks, famous for selling huge sandwiches. You treat yourself to one every week, so you stop for it before heading to war. The bus stop is packed with people struggling to get from one class to the next in less than twenty minutes. Class just let out and the nearby buildings leak students like blood, oozing them out onto the sidewalks as they puddle together where the buses stop. Beneath every bus stop overhang there is an electronic message board that flashes the time until the next bus arrives. There are ten minutes between buses and you know that it's going to be a dogfight. Every day it's a dogfight.

As the bus pulls down the street, people start drifting down the sidewalk trying to guess where it will land so that they stand a chance at pushing their way on. You manage to get onto the bus, which is packed to the point where the doors struggle closing. Your face is pressed right up against someone's The North Face logo on their back right shoulder.

The buses are always loud, but today they are louder than usual. Word is starting to spread. A young man—a student from the school—has committed suicide by jumping off of a large bridge. The news rips through each person and tears its way through the mindlessness of Tuesday. No one knows what to say or who to believe, but the news trucks that roam up and down Main Street and University Ave say enough. Channel 2, Channel 4, Channel 5, Channel 7—all send representation. Now we feel like celebrities—confused celebrities—in a sad world where bad news makes good news.

You're thankful to make it back to your dorm, where you try to reflect on the meaning of life, but in the room next to yours there is screaming, moaning: "Oh, Daddy, right there, Daddy."

The boy that lives next door is quite popular. You wonder what could drive a person to shout that. The apple you ate yesterday is turning brown on the window-sill.

Tonight is Two-Dollar-Tuesday at the bars off of Main Street. If you ever want to feel like a hero, go with a group of four friends to Two-Dollar-Tuesday. For ten dollars you can buy a whole round of drinks. Each person in the group will buy a round, so the rest of the night your drinks feel free, even though you've already paid for them. The rum doesn't hit you until everyone is done buying drinks. Somehow, you wake up the next day half-naked in bed with your clothes thrown about the room. But you're not going anywhere tonight because you have an exam on Friday that you are determined to study for.

WEDNESDAY

Today is a light day. You have one class in the morning and then your suicide prevention help group at night.

On the large lawns between classroom buildings there are hundreds of pounds of extra PVC pipe piled, squared off by caution tape. These are real eyesores. The University is always under construction somewhere, always inconveniencing its students with rerouted buses and closed-off parking lots. It is impossible to hide all of this caution tape from those high school tour groups, from your parents. The University is, however, able to sell it as progress. *Always building, always modernizing, so that we have the latest technology, the best of everything.* As if constant destruction and reconstruction is something to be proud of.

Viewing progress can make you thirsty, so it's time to cash in on one of your best kept secrets. When you buy a soda out of the vending machines, if you press the button twice really fast, two sodas fall out. Two Pepsis for the price of one. Back in your room, the refrigerator is full, because your roommate keeps stealing milk from the dining hall, stocking up on it, which you understand because you, too, are trying hard to get your money's worth at college.

After class you head back to your dorm and take the elevator up to the eighth floor, where you sit in the empty community lounge. On the bulletin boards in each floor lounge, the RAs have written *Rules For Living* that the students of each floor came up with together at the meetings on those first days of the fall semester.

1 - Don't be weird.
2 - Courtesy flush.
3 - Don't slam doors.
4 - Obey quiet hours.
5 - No stalking.
6 - Be a family.
7 - Make good stories, not good decisions.

There are no screens on the windows of the eighth floor lounge. Outside, to the left of the window are iron rungs along the brick wall, leading up to a flat roof where steam escapes the building. You texted a friend of yours who lives on another floor to meet you here and when she arrives you convince her to climb out the window with you. Between each ladder rung, there are spider webs that untangle at your touch. They stick to your fingers and you hate the way they feel on your skin, but there is a strange joy in being someplace where no one has been in a while. The two of you could stay up on the roof for weeks without anyone even realizing you were gone from your routines, just watching airplanes scar the blue sky with their fuel trails.

She places something in your hand: a silver marker. You glance at your cellphone for the date before you each write your names next to one another's on the roof.

This is a story you share with your support group.

"This is something, I think everyone should do," you say.

The group leader asks you how it made you feel to write your name up on that roof.

"Infinite," you say.

"Just like Charlie in *The Perks of Being a Wallflower*?" the girl with heavy makeup and scars on her wrists asks.

"Yes, exactly like Charlie."

You look around the circle, see the resilience of hope.

There's the middle-age hippie-cowboy, with a gray ponytail and large square-framed glasses that wanted to be a country singer. There's the bulimic whose wife left him after she found jars of vomit tucked away in the corners of their closet. There's the fourteen-year-old who sneaks away from his parents each Wednesday to join the group and talk about the bullies that torment him for being gay. These people talk about how they have had the ropes around their necks, the pills and guns in their hands. But you see the light of unfinished dreams in their eyes.

You notice the open window, a gross oversight, all things considered. The meeting is only on the third floor in an old office building, but the height just might be good enough.

When you came to your first meeting you wondered what you were doing here, but it didn't take long to understand why you came. One look and you could tell that these people understood destruction. You aren't suicidal anymore. And it's because you've already missed your chance. You've already lived through too much fucked up shit. If you were going to off yourself you should have done it after the car accident that left you with this horrible scar on your face. Or right after your mother died and left you parentless.

Pain is the well of strength.

And it is what keeps you going.

THURSDAY

One exam matters so little in the scheme of your life, but it feels like the most important thing in the world while you're trying to study.

When you look back at the past, years from now, that exam tomorrow will consider itself lucky to be a minor blip on the radar of things that mattered. Someone down the hall is playing music. People that were smart enough to arrange their schedules with Fridays off pass by your door, headed for the party. You know that when you look back on college, your social experience will matter more than the grade you get on tomorrow's exam. You slam your textbook, slide your feet into your shower-sandals and walk toward the music.

Dorm drinking is one of the greatest experiences at college—proves that time does fly when you're having fun.

Beer pong rules the night. You and your partner were good tonight, 7-0 good, and soon the two of you are headed for the lunch trucks—which are open late Thursdays and on the weekends. You're ready to devour a sandwich that you will wake up tasting, but won't remember eating. Halfway there, however, you both realize that you need to pee. The student center is closed after twelve and all doors are locked. Back and forth down

Main Street, the two of you pull at the handles of every dorm and classroom building, without luck. Unable to wait any longer you find a bush beneath an inconspicuous streetlamp and feel that sweet relief.

When the night is over, you find yourself back in your room, pulling a pillow over your eyes, breathing in through your nose and out through your mouth. Satisfied, your body sprints toward sleep.

Please evacuate the building. Attention, this is a real emergency. Please proceed to the nearest exit. Do not use the elevator. Repeat: do not use the elevator.

You debate whether or not to even get out of bed. If it's a real fire, you hope you'll be rescued. If you keep all lights off and lie still, they might not check to see if you've left the room, but they'll fine you and give you a hard time if they catch you not evacuating during a drill. Half-asleep and fully intoxicated, you flail for your phone and room key in the dark. You and everyone else stumble down the stairs, where you will wait for the next hour, shivering in the brisk spring night, for the fire department to clear the building for re-entry. Some kids thought it would be funny to grab fire extinguishers and shoot themselves down the hallway in rolling desk chairs.

It's three-thirty in the morning, which means this should technically be part of Friday. But since it still feels like Thursday in your mind, it will be remembered as such. You look around for someone else in your condition and the first thing you see is a group of kids with notebooks who've been up all night studying in the lounge.

People start moving back inside, herded like buffalo by ticked-off firefighters. At the entrance to every dorm building there is a sticker in the window that reads *Cameras for Safety*. Many people express their displeasure with their middle fingers toward the cameras as they re-enter.

FRIDAY

This time it's your alarm—a planned alarm—that wakes you. Hung over, you move to the bathroom, where you vow off alcohol. But it's okay because you know you don't mean it.

While on the toilet, one cotton-mouthed yawn follows another and you feel like a fire breathing dragon. Stray pieces of a phrase begin to wave in your head, strands of something witty that you feel a real need to tie together. *I left yesterday behind me and met today last night.* You repeat the words over and over to yourself so you don't lose them. They seem like song lyrics, but they aren't. Google confirms this on your phone in the bathroom. These words, you conclude, are a product of your own mind, a new motto that will make next week go by even faster. You're proud of this. You say this to yourself as you take the exam that matters less now than ever.

No one is responding to your texts. You want to know if your friends are going out tonight. Tiny insecurities slither into the cracks of your self-confidence. Why aren't they answering?

Everyone is still tired from last night, so nothing will happen tonight. Everyone will sit home in front of the TV, with Facebook open and music playing in the background.

After falling asleep somewhere during the night, you awake in the early morning. It's not yet four o'clock, a rare time when the sun and moon both seem to be on break. You throw a hoodie, sweatpants, and your glasses on and begin walking down the vacant streets toward a convenience store. About a mile into the journey, you find a ten dollar bill soaking face down in a sidewalk puddle. The dark green tree leaves hiss as you pick it up and decide to buy lottery tickets with it. There are streetlights every fifty feet or so down the road that connects The University to the nearby town. With your hood up and hands buried deep in your pockets, you walk into the store, where the man behind the counter shuffles toward the register.

"Morning."

You flip your hood off so that he can be easy, and you pick up a bag of Doritos and ask for five one-dollar scratch offs.

"Can I borrow a quarter?" you ask.

"You can have a penny. Maybe it'll be lucky." He points to the free pennies in the small tin on the counter. You take one and get to work on your lottery tickets. To your surprise, you don't win. No one ever wins at those things.

SATURDAY

In the early afternoon, you wake up with your breath smelling like Doritos. The aroma of weed lures you out into the hallway, where there are crumpled up beer cans leaning against the base of the wall where the cinderblock meets the carpet. Everything is quiet.

Some people, including your roommate, went home for the weekend yesterday, and those that are still around are sleeping because they have friends that answered their phones and were able to go hard last night. The damage doesn't lie. The bulletin board has been stripped of all paper. The naked corkboard stares at you—makes you feel dirty for looking at it. There are gobs of spit in the elevator. Half-dried, half-wet, puddles high in alcohol content. There is a used condom on the floor of the bathroom next to the paper towels that missed the wastebasket.

Tonight, you're going out for one reason. The bars are full of horny sorority girls who are eager to cram a lifetime of excitement into these four years because they know, even at this age, that they will look back on these days to prove to their older selves that their lives weren't always so mundane.

Weston Avenue is always crawling the final weekends before the end of the Spring Semester. When you arrive at Steel Tracks the place is packed.

You see a girl you like in a track jacket, leaning against the large mirror that makes the place look twice as crowded. There is a musty smell in the air as people dance. On your way to the girl, you pass a forty-year-old man sticking his straw into the drinks of people who aren't looking. When you get to her, there is a glow on her forehead. Beads of sweat shine in the fluorescent lights. From a distance, she may have been an angel, but as you approach, your opinion of her does a one-eighty.

"…I just think that if everyone stopped fighting there would be peace. It's that simple."

Standing there with your arms at your side, you allow her to continue. She's talking loud, trying to impress her friend who isn't listening. At first, you consider letting her get away with it, but you can't help yourself.

"There will never be world peace."

"Excuse me, but that kind of narrow thinking is exactly what prevents peace."

You wonder who she's trying to impress now because her friend left the moment you opened your mouth, eager for a distraction that would allow her to slip away without being a bitch.

"Nice jacket," you lie to her face. It's a high school jacket and it's pathetic. It has to have been at least three years since she has done any cheerleading.

"Mommy still cut your hair?"

She's quick to be harsh on you, to grab onto any flaw that she can find. She's looking for any excuse not to sleep with you because she's afraid of making those memories. Soon, however, you're walking through the crowd of people, glancing back over your shoulder to see if she's still following you toward the side exit.

SUNDAY

In the morning, she is as eager to leave as you are to see her go. You don't even bother to get her number—you don't even know her first name. If you should see each other around campus there is an implied understanding that this never happened.

You spend most of the day on your computer hoping a seat in the Philosophy class you want to take next fall will open up. You tried to get in when the web registration for next semester began weeks ago, but it's rare to get into all the classes you want on the first try. It's rare to get everything you want on the first try.

By the time the sun goes down, you're ready for some fresh air and a walk.

Outside the student center, there is a homeless man picking half-smoked cigarette butts off the sidewalk because when you're poor, you can't afford to have shame. You continue past the dilapidated dorms that they stick the freshmen in. Those buildings have seen so much. You wonder which rooms have had beer pong tables and parties in them. Which rooms have seen fucking and which have been fed a steady diet of virgins? It would be amazing if a light could tell you this. In the rooms that have had beer pong, a yellow light. In the rooms that have had sex, a blue light. A green light would appear for those rooms that had seen both, and darkness would remain for those that have been unfortunate enough to see neither. You wish you could do this with one snap of the fingers, revealing some of the school's most important history just like that.

Yellow.

Blue.

Green.

Just like that.

Sunday nights used to be hell in grade school. They were surrounded by dread and anxiety. Tonight is different. There is a happiness in every breath, a satisfaction in every step, a peacefulness to every eye blink.

Tomorrow is Monday, and Mondays matter to everyone in the world except for those in college.

I Really Wish You Weren't

"LOOKS LIKE I'M LATE," Courtney said to me.

"It's okay," I said.

"I'm really sorry, baby."

"Don't be. People are late every day."

It was spring and The University was alive. Girls who had been inside studying all winter made their way outside to reward themselves for months of hard work with a few hours of sunbathing. Guys who had been inside playing video games put the controllers down long enough to come outside, take their shirts off, and throw footballs around so the girls could watch.

Courtney had long brown hair, athletic legs, straight teeth, and a round button nose. Her skin was so white that the sun forced me to squint when it hit her at certain angles. Sliding her feet out of her sandals to rub my legs, she reached out, taking one of my hands between both of hers. We were seated on the hill overlooking the common courtyard of the Main Street dorms, she with her back against a tree and I with my back against her chest. As she wrapped her legs around me I turned my head back and looked into her eyes. They were watery, glossy mixtures of fear and happiness.

"People are late every day," I repeated. "We're here now…together…that's all that matters."

THE GIRL THAT MADE MY adolescent life a living hell sat across from me in Sunday school.

The devil works in mysterious ways.

She used to smile at me from across the circle and I would smile back, as a priest-in-training sat in the middle singing songs about God and playing the guitar. That was as far as anything ever went until eighth grade.

Alex, short for Alexandra—way too good of a name for her—had misleading green eyes and fire red-hair. She was tall, had a long nose, and too many teeth in the front of her mouth that turned every smile into a sneer. When I met her in second grade CCD, I was too stupid to run and oblivious to the fact that she liked me. During the eighth grade winter dance, her friend Gurt came up to me while I stood along the padded walls of the gymnasium with a group of friends, and asked me point-blank, "Matthew, do you like Alex?"

Gurt smiled at me the way a magician does before the prestige. She was chubby and her face was demonic. Feeling pressure from all eyes to answer, and ignorant of the true meaning of the question, I said, "Yes."

I meant that I liked her as a friend.

Sometimes all the devil needs is a misunderstanding to carry out a plan.

Later that night, my phone rang. It was Alex, over at Gurt's house with a group of girlfriends that were huddled up around her while we talked. She kept me on the phone for almost three hours, listening to the dry air through the phone lines, talking about nothing.

"So…well, it was nice talking to you," she said.

"It was nice talking to you, too."

"Welllllll…"

I knew what was expected of me. "Alex."

"Yes?"

I felt as if I had no other choice. "Will you be my girlfriend?"

"Yes!"

We both hung up the phone, she feeling giddy—as victors do after they have pursued and conquered something—and I feeling deceived, suffering a loss too faint to pinpoint in my heart, overwhelmed with apprehension.

BREATHING THROUGH OUR NOSES, Courtney and I sat there together without saying much, getting high on the trees that smelled like sex.

"Finished," she said, tucking a lock of hair behind her ear.

Lost in the moment, I hadn't even realized that she had been drawing on my hand.

"What do they mean?" I asked, wiggling my fingers.

She had drawn a different symbol above the nail on each, just below where the third knuckles bent. They were simple, miniature reminders of monumental things.

"This arrow," which was drawn on my index finger, "is so when you point to something you want, you know that it's okay to go after it and follow your dreams."

I flexed the finger, pointed toward the sky.

"The middle finger has a peace sign, to remind you to always be peaceful."

I leaned back to kiss her cheek. "The heart on the ring finger, to remember to love?"

She nodded. "And the smiley face on your pinky is to remind you to smile. And so you always have a friend."

I took the pen from her lap and replicated each picture on her fingers, adding a small "†" on her thumb.

"What's this one?"

"A cross to remind you to have faith that things will work out for the best, no matter how bad they seem."

Courtney grabbed my bangs, pulled my head back, and slid her tongue into my mouth. She found my thumb and held it still so that she could blindly draw the cross on it. The wind blew hard and a loose leaf fell. Strange, every flower was blooming.

She pressed her ear to my back, pulling me tight, and I could tell that she could hear my heartbeat because her fingers tapped my abdomen synchronically with every thump.

ALEX WAS AS EMO AS THEY CAME. She wore her hair short and spikey, or low over her eyes. Her nails were always painted black, and her lipstick shifted from shades of red and pink to blacks and grays as she progressed through grade school. She wore baggy black nylon pants with chains on them, and the entire first week after we started going out, I avoided her like the plague. We didn't have any classes together—she wasn't smart enough to get into honors classes—but she always found me at lunch. Day after day, she would sit on my lap, crushing my nuts while I ate, feeling much heavier than she looked. Every day before going to the cafeteria, I would come up with a list of possible things that we could talk about: the weather that day, my trip to the Grand Canyon the previous summer, school, the forecasted weather for tomorrow—anything to make the awkward silences less suffocating.

"Can't believe how hot it is out today."

She'd nod her head and say, "Uh, huh."

Without fail, I burned through my list of conversation topics to get me through to the bell, sweet merciful release, when Earth Science would come to my rescue. She just sat there, watching me eat, siphoning joy from me with her horrible personality.

She began hanging out with my friends and me after school, finding any excuse she could to piss all over whatever it was that we were doing, forcing all of us to sit on the curb in front of my house, staring at each other because she was boring as fuck.

"You want to play truth or dare?" Trevor suggested one day.

I shot him an angry look and he smiled back at me, intending to have his fun no matter what it meant for me.

"Yeah, let's do that," everyone agreed.

"No, that's lame," I said, but it was too late. It had already been decided.

I knew what they were going to dare me to do before the game even started.

"Matt, I dare you to kiss Alex."

She brought her face close to mine and forced her tongue down my throat. It was all I could do to keep from gagging. I could feel her teeth on my tongue as she opened and closed her mouth on mine.

The fact is she repulsed me. I made up an excuse a few minutes later, claiming that I needed to get ready to go out to dinner with my mom's friends from work, and when I went inside, I went straight for my toothbrush. I scrapped my tongue with the rough bristles until it bled, swirled mouthwash through my teeth, rinsing and spitting over and over until my mouth ran dry.

It didn't matter though, I still felt violated.

The more I relived it, the more nauseous I grew until I was dry heaving in the bathroom sink. After composing myself enough to get up to my room, I lay on the floor, hugging my knees to my chest, pulling myself into a tight ball, coping with the mind-rape the best that I could.

Two weeks later it was Halloween, the last Halloween where I planned to go trick-or-treating because I knew I was getting too old for it.

"Let's go," I said to Alex.

"I don't feel like going."

"Why not? Let's just go up and down the street real fast. I really want to."

"I'm not going." She crossed her arms over her chest on Trevor's basement couch.

"I guess we'll just stay in and watch TV," Trevor said.

So we sat there for two hours, doing nothing on one of the last nights I knew I could still feel like a kid.

"I'm going trick-or-treating," I said.

I got up and left. The guys in the group followed. The girls trailed a hundred feet behind us as we walked down the middle of the dim side street. From behind, I could hear Alex bitching.

"I don't want to go. I don't know why I'm going. Why are we walking out here?"

"Because I want to go and I'm tired of being miserable with you."

She gave me a *how dare you* look. "If you want to go trick-or-treating so badly, fine, but walk away and you're walking away from us."

Us. That bothered me more than being force-fed her tongue. I kept walking ahead with my friends.

Before we turned the corner, I looked over my shoulder at her and said, "I'd rather die than be with you."

"Oh, you'll be fucking sorry," she said.

"MAYBE WE SHOULD GET A PUPPY," I suggested to Courtney.

"My friend Melissa works with The University raising Seeing Eye dogs. I could ask her where they get their puppies from. Or maybe they know a breeder who could sell us one."

She and I had been living together since the end of junior year. The night she moved her stuff in, we took a shower together, christening one another while a bottle of Montrachet chilled in a bucket of melting ice in the bedroom. We drank it, both of us still soaking wet, wrapped together in one large towel, as the water took its time evaporating from our bodies. Strings of her hair stuck together in clumps, forming thick strands. I touched them, breaking them between my fingers.

With my hand resting on her shoulder, I drew closer and lowered my head, taking in the smell of her shampoo. She exhaled and I could smell the expensive wine on her breath. Something inside me ached for her. I grabbed her hips as her lips found my neck over and over. We collapsed into one another, pressing our bodies into the hardwood floor ravenous, unhindered by pain tempered by passion.

All of a sudden she stopped moving. Her eyes on my face, pupils dilating—unblinking with concentration—she placed her hand on my cheek and began running her fingertips up and down my long diagonal scar.

I must have winced. She asked, "Am I hurting you?"

"Please…don't stop."

My face began to burn where our skin met. I liked that it hurt. It felt as if she were healing it—healing it with her magic fingers.

"Blink," she said. And when I did, my cheeks were wet and my vision blurred.

Rays of gold and orange poured through the blinds, mixing with limb and skin in a fleeting, picturesque moment as the sun went down and we turned into one gray ball in the wake of dusk. *Please don't stop* was all I could think. *Please never stop.*

"A puppy would be fun," she said.

"Good practice, too."

THE WEEK AFTER I BROKE up with Alex, an openly gay kid at school asked me out. I let him down as easy as I could, but he seemed surprised when I said, "No." I should have put things together when that happened, but ignorance once again hindered my ability to make an important connection. It took something a little more blunt, more painful, to realize what was going on.

"I always knew you were a fag," this kid Frank said to me. He was someone I'd been friends with until he decided I was full of myself and began giving me a hard time. "All goody-goodies are fags. I knew you had to be one."

Caught off guard, a hard blush indicated guilt and gave him confidence as I stared back, not knowing what to do.

"You checking me out, little bitch? You want some of this? I'll give you some."

"I get girls all the time." A lie, but it was the only thing I could think of and something needed to be said.

"Oh yeah? Like who, puss?"

The truth was Alex was my first girlfriend. Hers was the only name I had to throw at him.

"Alex Brandt."

"You hooked up with Alex Brandt? Now I've lost all respect for you."

The fist he was about to hit me with dropped to his hip and I understood why. The thought of me kissing Alex Brandt was pathetic. Admitting it was painful enough and Frank knew that. As he walked away, I like to think that he realized I was suffering much more than anyone knew, and that I felt every bit as pathetic as I must have looked, standing there with my ironic defense.

It wasn't long before I felt like the whole school was watching me. Friends I'd had my whole life stopped talking to me. I felt like melting into myself, like crying my eyes out in someone's arms, but there was no one there for me. Every fiber in my body desired to stay home, to hide, to avoid the cruelty of others. But I dragged myself out of bed and went back to school each day. I pretended that I was okay. This bravery was rewarded in time. Most people soon realized that it was nothing more than a rumor. Some of my friends even began talking to me again, all of them in silent, mutual agreement never to bring the situation up. But the devil had done her damage.

The cruel thing about self-confidence is that it can take a lifetime to rebuild, yet a second to destroy.

———

COURTNEY'S FRIEND MELISSA gave us the name of a breeder thirty miles south of campus that had a reputation for turning out well-behaved, intelligent dogs.

"Might be a bit expensive," she told us.

"Money's not an issue."

"Well, then that's the place to go. Ask to speak with Rico when you get down there. Tell them Melissa Zhan sent you."

Courtney and I took Weston Avenue down to the train station, passing by empty shops with For Rent signs in the windows and some abandoned, run-down frat houses that kids used to enjoy sneaking into. Tiny grass blades peaked out of every crack in the empty parking lots we passed. On the front porch of one of the houses was a group of kids sitting in a semi-circle, cross-legged—their fingertips stained yellow, smoke betraying their breaths. Avoiding eye contact, I flipped my hood up and put my arm around Courtney as we walked.

On the train, we watched strangers come out of nowhere, stare at nothing, get off at their stop, and fade back into oblivion. A young man, no older than either of us, sat in the seat across the aisle, playing with his pocket watch.

"I've never actually seen someone with a pocket watch before," Courtney whispered.

"I know, right?"

I leaned across the aisle, extending my head into the neutral space. "Hey buddy, what time is it?"

His eyes brightened. Fumbling with the watch, forgetting how it worked while under pressure, he looked from us to the watch to make sure we didn't disappear before he could answer. Finally opening it, he said, "Two-thirty."

"Thanks."

"Nice watch," Courtney said.

"Thanks. My dad gave it to me."

He seemed happy that we'd given him a chance to use it. Roused from whatever he had been thinking about, it was like he'd just drank a large cup of coffee. As the three of us traded small talk, I got such positive vibes from him that it made me sad. I hoped he had someone to love him. I turned away, stared out the window, watched the graffiti on buildings go by as fast as life. When we reached our stop, Courtney and I got off, two strangers to the other passengers fading into our own oblivion.

"We'd like to speak to Rico please," Courtney said when we got to the breeder's lobby. The receptionist at the desk began to say something but was cut off by a thin, lanky man in a gray tuxedo. He had wispy white hair that matched his shoes.

"Rico's not in, but I'm more than capable of helping you. I'm Maxwell. Co-owner. I've been running this business with Rico for over twenty years."

Courtney looked at me, asking *What should we do?* with her eyes. I nodded.

"That's fine, Maxwell. What kinds of dogs do you have?" I asked.

"All kinds, sir. Labrador retrievers, beagles, terriers, basset hounds, Danes, Dobermans, Rottweiler, Siberian huskies, pugs, poodles, goldens, dachshund, collies. Anything in particular you're looking for?"

I began to see why we'd been told to ask for Rico.

Courtney looked over at me, smiling. "That's quite an impressive selection."

"How about we start with Labs?" I asked.

"Yes, excellent choice, sir. Labradors are our most popular. Very intelligent. Very loyal. Excellent temperament. Very smart. Damn near almost human."

Perfect.

He walked us through long, well-lit hallways that resembled a hospital's. We passed rooms full of older dogs housed in what looked like plastic cubbies—no cages, no bars in this world.

"Here we are," he said, "the lab room. Feel free to watch them play, see how they interact. Observe their demeanor. Interact with them yourself, if you'd like."

The room was sectioned off into six square cube-pens that separated the puppies by litter. Maxwell watched us as if we were the puppies. His razor slash lips peaked upward at the corners. When we felt like we'd placated him enough, Courtney reached down and picked up a puppy. He was a yellow Lab with a strange brown tip to his tail, as if it had been dipped in chocolate on the day he was born and it had remained, a tattoo.

"You hold him," she said, extending her arms, passing the pup to me like he was a priceless vase.

Everything about him was miniature. He had kind, thoughtful eyes. He was calm, studying the world from his perch in my hands. I massaged his paws, which were a few sizes too big for him. After pressing my nose to his, he licked my upper lip with a small sandpaper tongue. His breath smelt new.

"I lovvvve him," Courtney beamed.

I ran my hand up and down the puppy's forearm as if to say, *You're ours now*, and when I did, I was surprised when his du-claws scratched me.

"I lovvvve him, Matt. We could call him Split because he looks like a banana split!"

"Split," I said to him.

Split licked his nose, unaware of what was happening.

"Yes, then, very good. I must say, I love working with younger people. They always fall in love with the first thing they see. It's quite precious. Makes me love my job."

Maxwell took Split from me and walked out of the room to get him ready. As soon as he was gone, Courtney jumped me with kisses.

"You're pretty when you smile. You should do it more often." She took my head between her hands. "I'm gonna fix you, Matthew."

"Promise?"

"I promise."

THERE ARE MULTIPLE LIES to every truth, injustices for every good deed. Maybe someone somewhere was benefitting from my suffering. Maybe I was paying my dues early, so that one day I would know what I had in Courtney. Either way, trouble is always easier to find than it is to lose.

Six weeks after she realized that Plan A had failed, Alex turned to Plan B: telling everyone at school that I had gotten her pregnant.

"I can't believe you fucked her!" Frank yelled at me in front of everyone in the cafeteria.

"I didn't do it."

Turning to the kids around him, with his arms out past his shoulders, he said, "Yeah right. Did you see the size of her stomach?"

Alex really was pregnant.

"Her stomach's ballooning up already. You sick fuck. What are we, 13? That kid's going to come out retarded!"

Right after I broke up with her, Alex started dating a high school man-child named Damon. Damon had flat-topped black hair that was so short you could see every blemish on his scalp. Trevor pointed to the picture in his older sister's high-school yearbook after we followed Alex home one day after school. We watched her get into Damon's black coupe. Saw him drive away, swerving, as Alex's head bobbed up and down in his lap. Row after row of grinning, youthful faces came to a crashing halt at Damon's stoic mug in the yearbook. Like a man with a secret that he was prepared to take to the grave, his mouth was flat, his face expressionless. A five o'clock shadow gave his cheeks a leathery look, like a reptile's. They made a perfect match and would make perfect demon babies together that would grow up to torment the world, to hurt innocent people and smile while they did it.

"I didn't sleep with her" became my motto.

I offered these same five words to all the kids that stared at me. Relationships I'd worked on for years were decimated beyond repair. Teachers questioned me, grilled me as if I were a hardened criminal. The school called my mom, dragged her into it, even though she was weak and ill. I stole a handle of Absolut vodka from the liquor cabinet—considered killing myself with it. Would that even make Alex sorry for what she'd done? I doubted it. While Frank was shouting at me that day at lunch, I saw Alex across the cafeteria, grinning from ear to ear, laughing at me and pointing with that same friend who'd tricked me into saying that I liked her. My life was a game to her.

I returned the bottle before anyone ever noticed, but I liked knowing that it was there. In the midst of it all, I felt like I'd won something when I came to grips with the fact that I was a loser.

TINY BLINKING LIGHTS of distant boats betrayed the horizon in the dark.

"Take my shirt."

The three of us had spent the day at the beach together. The warmth of the sun was replaced by the coldness of the moon. I handed her my t-shirt and she slid it over her black tank top. "Thanks."

Split bounced from her lap to mine. Courtney's hip brushed against my hand and goosebumps blanketed my body. My nipples got hard as she traced an arrowed-finger in circles over the left one. Our puppy nuzzled my chest with his head, doing his best to warm me.

"I really wish you weren't just late," I said.

Courtney gave a full belly sigh before lying on her back, offering, "Me, too" toward the stars.

I leaned back next to her on the sand, both of us staring up at the infinite sky, considering all that might have been.

While Courtney thought of baby names, I thought of how one morning, after waking up too many days unhappy with my life, I had decided to change it. The day I made a conscious decision to stop giving a fuck about other people freed me from their malice. And somehow, through interpersonal disconnect, despite my justifiable bitterness, Courtney had found me.

It had been years since I had thought about the future with such hope. A baby would have given life meaning.

Split had fallen asleep between us, his head resting on Courtney's breast, a well-proportioned pillow. Through closed eyes we imagined an unfocused, hazy life together. The world spun us. We extended our outer arms and together made an angel in the sand.

Anywhere

J ESSICA WAS STILL FIXING her makeup in the bathroom. The rest of us were sitting in the living room of my apartment wondering what the fuck had just happened.

"Get your feet off the table," I scolded Scuzzy.

"Oh, man, I'm so sorry," he said.

Jessica came back to the room, sat down in one of the leather armchairs, pulled out her phone, and started texting.

"I'm going to kill myself," her boyfriend Jake said.

"Easy," I told him, but I couldn't blame him.

He'd been with Jessica for four years, high school sweethearts who'd chosen The University so that they could stay together. He'd given up a track scholarship for her and she'd repaid him by going down on our friend Chalkie in my bathroom.

"I should have never gone to check on her," Jake said.

Chalkie had left right after he got off, taken the back door out before I could stop him and ask him why he'd done it.

"You're so pathetic," Jessica said to Jake.

"I still love you," he said.

She was still wearing his ring, so I thought they may have a chance.

"Tell me to go fuck myself. Tell me to go to hell. To get away from you. That you never wanna see me again."

"It is what it is," he said.

"So pathetic."

All I wanted to do was paint. Inspiration strikes like a blind boxer, its punches random and off-center. There was no way they were going to let me put brush to canvass before it faded.

"I really wish you had just gone to the bathroom," Jake said.

"You're so pathetic that I bet if I had you watch next time you'd just stand there."

I wasn't close with Jake but she was starting to get on my nerves.

Scuzzy stood up, staggered and fell backward, crushing the wicker chair he'd been sitting on.

He was trying to change the subject and I loved him for it.

"You fucking asshole," I shot up. "Those chairs belonged to my parents."

"Oh my God, dude, I'm so sorry," he said.

I winked at him and he turned it on real dramatic then, picked up the pieces and said, "I'll help you bury them."

Jessica stood up and left. The other girls followed and I began to think I may get to paint tonight after all.

"Scuzz, why don't you head to Corner Pub and I'll catch up with you in a little bit?" I asked.

"Sure thing, man," he said. He stacked the broken pieces of the chair into the corner, picked up an open beer, and left.

I had to make sure Jake didn't kill himself on my watch.

He picked up Jessica's unfinished beer and kissed the lip of the can where her lips had been.

The walls in the room were sky blue. Gray streaks from the sheetrock beneath shown through where the paint had faded. They looked like dirty clouds. The more we drank, the closer Jake and I felt. Alcohol and the company of a friend who understood that sometimes it's alright to feel sorry for yourself were the two things Jake needed most.

We started naming the shapes the gray clouds made.

"Revolver," I said pointing.

"Bullets," he answered.

"Those small ones?"

"Yes, the two of them."

"A kite," I said.

"Diamonds."

"Or two kites."

We continued like this for God knows how long. At some point, sleep crept in through the side window and overtook us both. When I woke up several hours later, Jake was nowhere to be found, and I was certain that life was a dream.

I FOUND SCUZZY AT Corner Pub, talking to a man with one leg.

"This is him now, man," Scuzzy said, slapping a hand on my shoulder.

The man was resting his nubbed knee on the barstool next to him as if it were a normal thing to do.

"Jake's gone," I said.

"Oh no, not good, man. That kid needs supervision."

"I know. He could be anywhere."

"I'll go check his apartment. I'll climb in through an open window if I have to," Scuzzy said.

He left me there to finish his beer. It was close to nine on a Saturday night and the place was empty. I could never quite figure out why kids avoided Corner Pub. It was the uncool place to be, and I enjoyed it very much.

"How'd you get that scar on your face," the one-legged man asked me.

"Knife fight," I told him.

He thought this over for a while, then nodded like he'd given me his blessing. I didn't ask him about his leg because I didn't care. This seemed to disappoint him, and he turned away from me toward the open room.

"I lost my leg working compost machinery," the man said. "Been out on disability for six months. When I came back, they canned my ass. Twenty years I worked there, wasting away my life. They said they'd found someone better at the job but we both know the real reason why they got rid of me."

"Don't they have lawyers for that? Wrongful termination, discrimination or some shit?" I asked.

The man shrugged his shoulders, waved his short leg back and forth, and gave a *what the fuck can I do?* look. From his pocket he pulled out a bag of dust.

"Want it?" He held the bag out to me in his left hand. "Sleep with me and it's yours. No woman wants to sleep with a man with one leg."

And a guy would?

I took the bag from him and ordered another drink. A half-hour later, the man strapped his prosthetic on and we left. We were walking to his car. I took off running just as he went to put his arm around me.

I tried calling Scuzzy but it went straight to voicemail and his inbox was full. Leaving a message with him would be pissing into the wind. And it was a windy autumn night. I popped my North Face collar up and put my hands in my pockets, headed for a sorority house, just off campus, where I knew a few of the easier girls.

The driveway was made of rocks, so I picked a handful up and threw them at Daisy's window. The sound of broken glass echoed off the tree leaves.

"Daisy!" I called out in mock longing.

A bright light went on and two girls looked down at me through the jagged pieces of glass.

"What the fuck, asshole?"

"Daisy, come down here."

"Go the fuck away."

"Look, Daisy!" I held up the bag of dust.

"There's no Daisy here, lunatic."

"Oh, sorry."

The beer I'd drank at my apartment had gone through me, I found a tree on the side of the house, pulled my dick out, and began to water it. Police sirens grew louder over drunk-kid-chatter down the street. Paranoid, I took off running through the back parking lot, my legs beginning to feel wet and warm as I flopped away.

In the lot behind the house, a bald man with a pencil-thin beard and green windbreaker rose from between two cars, startling me with a deep voice. "That for me or you?"

"Hell knows. Sirens are sirens." I shrugged.

"Zip that thing up." He pointed a screwdriver between my legs, then squatted down and got back to work on the door he was trying to open.

Half turning, I zipped my fly up and pulled the dust out of my pocket. I opened the top of the bag, moved my nose to the opening and took a careful sniff. My breathing calmed.

"Get in," the bald man said.

I noticed the gun when it caught the moonlight. He'd traded the screwdriver for a black 9mm piece with a silver handle. He pointed it at me and I right away thought of Jake, how he'd kill himself if I died before I could save him. I got in the car, the man wired it, and the engine roared to life.

"The sirens are getting louder," I said.

"Then you better hurry up and line that shit up. We ain't going anywhere till we hit some of that."

"Start driving and I'll line it up on the dash. When you're ready to snort, I'll hold the wheel for you."

This seemed to please him. He balled up his windbreaker and threw it at my feet. With the gun still in one hand he drove over the curb and onto the side street.

With unsteady hands I made two lines with the powder on the dashboard, leaned in, and inhaled one of them. The thief waited until we got on a straight road before telling me to take the wheel.

The car slowed below 25mph. He leaned his head down toward the dash. I made sure the doors were unlocked, made it look like I was reaching for the wheel, and threw what was left of the powder in his face. In one motion, I grabbed the windbreaker to help cushion the landing, opened the door, and rolled out of the car.

My shoulder took the worst of it. It jammed when I hit the pavement, and my forehead got scuffed, but I was okay. The stolen car swerved, red break lights lit up for a second, and then it drove on out of sight. I stood up and headed back to my apartment for my car.

NO ONE KNEW WHERE JAKE WAS.

"I don't really care where he is. Last I saw, he was with you," Jessica said over the phone. Whatever happened to him would be on me.

Chalkie wasn't answering my calls or texts, so I drove by his apartment to see if Jake had gone there looking for a fight. No one was home and the lights were off.

Up and down The University streets I went, hoping to spot him. What had he been wearing? It bugged me that I hadn't thought to notice. All I could remember was his shirt. A neon-lime-green Sun Drop soda t-shirt.

As I drove, I noticed the driver in the car to my right texting as we went down Main Street. He swerved and almost sideswiped me, looked up just in time to avoid taking the open door off of a Jeep as a woman got out. I decided to take matters into my own hands. It was the reason why I drove a beat up ninety-six Taurus when I could have driven a Porsche.

The look on his face was priceless. Utter disbelief that something bad had happened to him. I'd eased my silver tank into the whole left side of his Mazda.

"You'll fucking pay for this," he said as he got out of his car. He was mid-thirties, curly black hair down to his shoulders, teal, collared golf shirt that was a size too tight.

A cop pulled up in a few minutes and the officer was standing right next to me as the man fished his cell phone out from between the pedals.

"Important call, sir?" the officer asked.

The man stammered, searched for words, blamed me for the accident.

The woman he'd just missed killing came up and gave a statement. I pictured Jake jumping out in front of a car.

"Have there been any deaths tonight?" I asked the officer.

"No. Why do you ask?"

"Good," I said.

He kept a closer eye on me after that while he finished taking our information and filled out his report. A few weeks later, I received a check from Geico—Mazda man's insurance company—for three-hundred forty-four dollars and eleven cents.

AFTER THE SIDESWIPE, I parked my car in the student center parking lot and walked over to a fraternity house that was having a party. There were always hundreds of people packed into the common room of Kappa Something fraternity and this offered me a better chance of finding Jake.

There was a mob of kids trying to get in around back. In a few minutes I worked my way to the front, where two brothers were guarding the door, and I dropped Riley's name.

"How do you know Riley?" an overweight kid in a baggy t-shirt asked.

"He's a friend."

"Sorry, not good enough," he said. "Ratio's five-to-one and I don't see any girls with you."

Calling Riley wasn't an option. When the kid partied, he turned his phone off. You were either with him or you weren't when things got started. I looked up at the fire escape and decided that it was my best option, but just then, the back door swung open and another brother walked out with a girl on his arm. Back when I was a freshman, this place had recruited me hard. I'd seen the vice president of the chapter around campus and we'd been on good terms the few times we'd exchanged words.

"Yo, where's Riley?" I grabbed his free arm.

He leaned his head back as he tried to figure out where he knew me from. When he placed my face, he said, "Oh, hey man. Riley? He's in there somewhere. Kid was crowd surfin' earlier. You tryna get in?"

"Yeah but…" I rolled my eyes toward the overweight brother.

"Hey, Jimmy, let this kid in. He's fuckin' loaded."

"But—"

"You heard me, NIB. You see this guy, you let him in. Matt, right? Rose, like the flower. I'm on my way out right now but have a good time." He leaned in close and whispered in my ear, "It's wild in there. If you run into any trouble, tell them VP said you're *travelling* tonight. And seriously, bro, reconsider joining us."

After thanking him, I pushed past Jimmy and became part of the mosh that engulfed the large common room. Three-hundred sweaty college kids made the house twenty degrees warmer than outside. Black lights, glow sticks, and a few dozen cellphones were the only lights.

There was a DJ at the front of the room, a celebrity for the night, lifted to semi-fame by a small stage that put him on display. Behind the bar on the far wall, brothers passed out drinks to girls, demanded money from guys. I climbed up on the bar to get a better view. Drunk girls were dancing up there next to me. Horned up guys stood by, looking up their skirts, waiting to catch them if they fell. Jake's neon-green shirt would have stood out like a highlighter in a box of Sharpies if he were here.

"Get down, asshole."

"Ew, go away."

The girls dancing on the bar pushed me off. No one made an effort to catch me. I landed on my ankle funny, stumbled forward, and pushed myself up before I got trampled. The stairs that lead to the bedrooms were around the corner, if I couldn't find Jake, maybe I could find Riley and ask him if he'd seen or heard about a kid in a Sun Drop t-shirt at the party.

More security stopped me before I could go upstairs.

A short red-headed guy with acne pits crossed his arms and said, "Only brothers allowed up there, dude."

"I'm here to see Riley."

"I doubt he's looking to bring dudes up to his room."

The rest of the guys standing around laughed at me.

"VP said I'm travelling tonight."

Like magic, the expressions on their faces changed. The brothers parted to the sides, showed me the way up with open-palmed hands.

"Sorry, dude. What's your name, bro?"

"Matthew Rose."

"You should have led with VP. I was just joking with that gay crack before."

Grabbing the railing I pulled myself up the stairs. When I got to the top, I turned back and looked down at the redhead and asked, "What's a NIB?"

"Newly Initiated Brother." His face flushed.

I turned the corner and limped through the second floor labyrinth of dirty rooms until I found Riley's. He had spray-painted a shocker hand on his door that was hard to miss. There was loud music coming from inside, I pushed the door open and found Riley, Scuzzy, and a few other guys and girls downing a shot.

"Matty boy, what's up?" Riley lowered the music.

Scuzzy flushed hard when he saw me. "I'm sorry," he said. "He wasn't at his apartment. I tried, man, I really did."

"What happened to your face?" Riley asked. "Your forehead's been bleeding."

I told them about the car thief with the gun, the man in the Mazda, and the girls who'd pushed me off the bar downstairs.

"Sit down." Riley put a hand on my chest, guided me into his desk chair, and handed me a shot glass. "I'll help you feel better. We're killing handles. One shot every other minute while you're in my room. Get fucked up or get the fuck out!"

I stayed in Riley's room for ten minutes. No one there had seen Jake, either.

"I'll help you back to your place, man. You can barely walk." Scuzzy put his arm across my back, took the weight off my bum ankle.

"Hit me up, later," Riley said.

As we turned to walk away I heard one of Riley's friends say, "He's a lightweight, that one, huh?"

"Matt? No. He's just restless."

In the hallway, there were two people groping each other. A boy had a girl pressed against the wall. Both of his hands wrapped around her smaller wrists as he pinned her arms to the sides of her head. The girl responded by pulling her hips up to his, pushing herself onto her tiptoes as they kissed.

A side door opened to the fire escape and in a few minutes Scuzzy had me down on the ground again.

"You don't even know who you're dealing with! I'm with the Columbian mafia! You don't even know, son! My family's with the fucking Columbian mafia!"

A kid had been refused entrance and was screaming at the top of his lungs. He wore red high-rise sneakers, a gold chain with a circular emblem, a backwards flat-brimmed Yankees hat. He pounded his chest as his friends tried to pull him away from the house. A few of the fraternity brothers had gathered on the front porch and yelled back at him.

"Fuck you all! You're all dead! We're gonna come back and kill every single one of you motherfuckers!"

Jake.

How long had it been since we sat naming clouds and I'd last seen him? There were plenty of ways he could have offed himself in four or five hours.

"You don't really think he'd go through with it, do you, man?" Scuzzy asked.

I didn't have the heart to tell him that I did.

AT THE INTERSECTION OF Main Street and University Ave there was a little girl waiting to cross with her mother. The light changed, they stepped out into the street first and that's when they saw the bird.

"Don't touch it, Meesha. For God's sake, please walk!"

The child couldn't have been more than three years old. She was entranced by the broken beak and twitching feathers.

"Oh, for the love of God," the mother said, lifting the child off her feet, carrying her the rest of the way.

I pulled away from Scuzzy, bent down to pick up the dying bird, and ran as best as I could toward the little girl. Her eyes were wide balls of concern peaking over her mother's shoulder, staring at me.

"I have it, Meesha. I have him. Don't worry."

The mother half-turned, looked horrified at me.

"Leave us alone. Are you out of your mind?"

"He'll be okay, Meesha. I promise."

Meesha reached out for my hands, but her mother was too quick. She cradled the little girl, moving fast down the sidewalk.

"He'll be okay, I promise," I began stroking the bird's head, "I promise, Meesha."

I waited for the little girl to get out of sight, around the corner, before placing the bird in the nearest trashcan.

"That poor bird," Scuzzy said, helping me walk again.

"That poor little girl," I said.

"You have a beautiful heart, man."

But I didn't feel beautiful. I felt about as good as I looked. Scuffed. Bruised. Scarred.

Thank God we saw him first. A hundred feet ahead, the man with one leg leaned against a brick wall outside of Nightclub bar.

"We have to run," I whispered.

One thing about Scuzzy, when you tell him to run, he doesn't ask questions. He's smart like that. The one-legged man saw me, screamed "Stop!", and began to hobble after us with surprising speed. Scuzzy scooped me up in his arms and carried me the rest of the way back to my apartment. We'd gotten inside the back door without him seeing which building we'd gone into. From my kitchen, we stifled back laughs as we watched him look around the parking lot outside my window.

"Close call," Scuzzy said. "You're the king of them tonight."

Something about that word, stuck in the air. It hung like irony, annoying and sweet.

Close.

"Let's get you some ice." Scuzzy opened the freezer, cracked an ice cube tray, and filled a Ziploc bag.

"You're too kind," I said.

He blushed.

In a few minutes I was shivering.

"You need rest, man," Scuzzy said. "Let's get you up to bed."

He helped me out of my shoes and up the stairs. All at once I needed to crash. Whatever happened while I slept, I would have to live with. My shoulder ached, my ankle was twice the size it should have been.

We flipped the light on in my room, and found Jake. Curled up in a little ball under my comforter, the coward.

I didn't know whether to laugh or cry, so I did both.

Scuzzy checked his pulse. Gave me two thumbs up.

He hadn't gone anywhere.

He'd been right there the whole time.

The Trillion Dollar
Question

T HE SADDEST TIMES WERE when the red folders would show up out of nowhere. Like little knives that gave emotional paper cuts, those things did damage. This time it was a woman pushing a man in a wheelchair. She had one tucked under her arm and he had one open on his lap in front of him. The woman stopped beneath an oak tree, parked the man next to a bench, and I thought to myself *even they would do*.

Parent Orientation.

"Welcome to The University", the red folders read.

Just yesterday, it seemed, I was sitting in the gymnasium at my own orientation. The first thing The University had done was separate parents from students. The parents were ushered into the gymnasium to listen to the president and deans speak, while incoming freshman, like pebbles in a gutter washed downhill by an unexpected rain, were ushered down University Ave toward the lecture halls. It was there that we were divided into groups based on last name, sent to classrooms where we were given our own red folders and told to pick classes for our first semester.

I'll never forget that walk. University Ave was lined with upperclassmen cheering us on. They encouraged us and clapped for us while we made our way.

"Welcome to The University!"

"Look alive! Welcome home!"

"Smile! You're leaving your parents!"

Funny, the things that stick with us. How pain makes a memory feel more recent.

I turned away from the couple with the red folders. Walked into the dining hall and saw a poster advertising Midnight Breakfast. This made me feel a little better. It was a tradition that happened at the end of every semester, the dining hall stayed open late and served breakfast to students who were up studying for final exams. As I ate lunch alone, I looked up at the beautiful glass ceiling, saw the never-ending sky looking down on me. Did my best to forget about the red folders.

"NEVER MAKE EYE CONTACT," was the key rule I had broken. You're dead once you do and both of us knew it. I was on my way to class, walking down University Ave toward Maria Hall for my philosophy final. The man handed me a slip of paper, and to be polite, I took it. It was a trillion-dollar bill with a picture of the Liberty Bell on it. At first it looked like real money, but it lacked that rough feel, the paper was too smooth, and the message on the back betrayed it.

> *The trillion dollar question: Will you go to Heaven when you die? Here's your answer. Have you ever told a lie, as Satan would? Stolen anything? Used the Lord's name in vain? Jesus said, 'Whoever looks at a woman to lust for her has already committed adultery with her in his heart.' Have you looked with lust? Will you be guilty on Judgment Day? If you have done these things, God sees you as a lying, thieving, adulterer at heart. If you have chosen to live a life of sin, you have chosen to live an afterlife in hell.*

Hell must be crowded, I thought.

Shaking my head, I folded the phony bill and slid it into my pocket. The bus stop was crowded as usual. Kids jockeyed for position on the sidewalk, so close to the curb as the buses roared by that one slight push would have knocked three or four of them off balance and made national news. Inside Maria Hall, kids were sitting on top of one another and the heat of the room was unbearable. I left feeling indifferent about grades and irritated at people in general.

As I crossed back over the street, the crowd of kids waiting for the buses was facing the wrong direction, forming a half circle around that same man, who was standing on a milk crate preaching through a megaphone.

"You can all still be saved. Shun sin and your way of life. Deny Satan and beg Jesus for forgiveness!"

Half of the crowd of kids was laughing, exchanging *Is this dude really serious?* glances. The other half was mortified.

"When was the last time you've all been to church?" he snarled, his words echoing off the overhang of the bus stop.

Years.

"It's not too late to pray for salvation, to beg the Lord to unstain your souls. You don't have to spend eternity burning in hellfire so long as you spend the rest of this life repenting!"

Not in the mood to be spiritually threatened, I put my headphones in my ears and flicked on a song.

"You there! You with the Devilish scar on your face! Do you turn away from the Lord? So you choose Satan!"

An angel out of nowhere, Scuzzy stepped forward from the crowd.

"What the fuck, man? You leave him alone."

"Another sinner!" the man screamed into his megaphone. "Pray and repent! So you, too, shun Jesus?"

I believe there are moments when God gives you an absolute sign that you are in the right place, that you're exactly where he wants you to be in life at a specific time. Subtle, divine pats on the back.

This was one of those moments.

I meant to click the Pause button on my music but hit the Next button by mistake. "Heaven Can Wait" by Meat Loaf flashed across the screen. I tripped over a crack in the uneven sidewalk, would have landed on my scarred face, had Scuzzy not been there to catch me.

"Faggots!" cried the preacher, looming in the shadows of dusk with a disgusted snort. "What's worse than faggots?"

"Leave them alone, asshole," a girl from the crowd yelled out.

I put one hand on either side of Scuzzy's face and kissed him on the mouth.

Had I been worth a trillion dollars, I would have traded every penny for the look on the preacher's face. A few people laughed, many applauded. I put my head-phones back in my ears and headed back up University Ave.

"YOU'RE A GOOD KISSER, MAN," Scuzzy said.

"Shut up," I told him.

"Just saying, you've got the lips and the money, too. If you were a girl or I were into dudes…" He pulled out a cigarette and I held up a lighter to spark it for him.

"Such a gentleman, too." He inhaled hard, made the fire glow to life as we walked on. "You want one?"

"Nah, I don't feel like smoking," I said.

He coughed and spit into the street. I watched where it landed and saw something I'd never noticed before.

Bricks.

Scuzzy's spit had fallen into a small circle where the asphalt had been ripped away. Red bricks of a hidden past peaked out in the glow of a streetlamp.

"Have you ever noticed that all of your friends start with S?" Scuzzy asked.

"Huh?"

"S. Skeeter. Scuzzy. That guy Sash you always tell me about. I think you have a thing for the letter S. An S-fetish, man."

"You're certifiable."

"Guilty," he said.

He took his pocket knife out of his sock and carved "Matt loves S" into the nearest tree.

"Well, your name is William, not Scuzzy."

"Guilty again, man," he said. "Hey, why haven't I met Sash, anyway? His father sell drugs? Family have oil?"

I couldn't answer this. Some things are meant to always be secret.

"Hey-yo, S-boy."

"What is it, Scuzzy?"

"That ain't a bad thing, loving the letter S. I'm just saying, I'd still be your friend if you liked the letter T. Or Q. That'd be kind of weird though—Q—but I'd still be here for you, man."

It was at that moment that I realized I loved him. Not in an *I want to sleep with you* kind of way, but in a deeper way. Scuzzy was the only person alive who could always make me feel good. I didn't understand half the shit that went through his mind, but his soul was the elixir to my sadness.

"Would you still love me if my name didn't start with S?" he asked. But he didn't wait for an answer. He punched my arm and winked, dashed off down the sidewalk, and I headed for the church.

THE SHARP, TALL TOWERS of the Victorian church cut desperately into the night sky, black arrows toward heaven hidden in the navy-soaked dome. University construction cranes threatened the buildings around the church, but as every church seems to do, it sat stubborn and immune to modernity.

I walked in, sat down in the front pew, and Jesus apologized to me.

They don't know they embarrass you, do they? I asked him.

They mean well, he said from the cross.

Face to face, Jesus looked much nicer than the way the preacher had painted him.

It's good to see you, old friend, Jesus said.

His voice was loud and hearty and my bones shook to it. I looked up and he was silent, head bowed to one side, mouth half-open.

Real or unreal, God or son of God, there is something human in his face.

I'm still mad at you, I said.

I know, son.

Biting my bottom lip until the coppery taste of blood flooded my mouth, I held back everything I wanted to ask him because sometimes, even Jesus doesn't have a solid answer.

My attention shifted from the crucifix to the candles. Only one among the hundred was lit—a lone beacon of prayer surrounded by neglect. Something hung around its base. I stood up, walked over to it, picked up the rosary beads, and fingered them as my tears splashed on the marble at my feet, turning instantly—I imagined— into holy water. I pulled out two fifty-dollar-bills—real bills, ones without a single threat on them—and slid them through the donation slot. Borrowing the flame from the lone candle, I lit every last one of them and stood there for a few minutes, my face glowing, feeling more whole than I'd felt in years.

I left the church having connected with God in a personal way. No mass or formal ceremony can compete with that.

I found Scuzzy sitting on his porch with a ciga-rette in one hand and a hookah hose in the other.

"Fucking chimney," I smiled.

He laughed silently, his baggy t-shirt shaking—hiding his thin, malnourished bones. "Fucking chimney crickets!"

"You think we go to heaven when we die?"

His eyes widened, startled by the abruptness of the question. "You dying on me?"

"No." I handed him the trillion dollar bill, told him about my conversation with Jesus, the red folders, and the candles.

"There's no such thing as death," he said, waving his hand in the air and handing the bill back to me. "Man, I'll tell you what heaven really is. I've got a philosophy that clears all that shit up."

He handed me the hookah hose and I inhaled, bracing myself for one of his unintelligible, loosely woven rants.

"You wanna hear it?" he asked.

"Sure, why not?"

"My theory is that each star is really the same star. Let me explain, man. Each star is our own star. And each star in the sky, in the universe, is our own solar system duplicated. Over and over again."

Scuzzy sat back in his folding chair, put his feet up on the porch railing, and took a deep, satisfied drag from his cigarette.

"So how does that explain heaven and death?"

"We live the same lives over and over in those parallel universes for infinity. When we die, there is no heaven or hell. We go live in one of those other universes, around another star. When we lose consciousness for good in this solar system, our eyes open—as the same person—in another. This may be why some things—some people—feel familiar to us, man, even though they're completely new to this particular life. Who knows how many times you and me have had this same conversation? That's why we'll never be able to travel too far in space. Those other lives are just out of reach. Death here though gets us there instantly. Dead relatives are still with us because we really are still with them, man."

"So it's just the same thing over and over again?"

"No, not exactly. There are slight variations. Every solar system is a different choice you made in your life. So maybe around one star I'm an alcoholic, maybe I'm a valedictorian, maybe you never get into that car accident and don't have that scar on your face, maybe your dad makes it out of that building and your neighbor gets cancer instead of your mom."

I took the cigarette from his hand and smoked it down to the filter. Scuzzy looked at me with pained eyes, hoping he hadn't upset me. I'd never heard anything like his philosophy before.

"Go on…what else?"

When he saw that I wasn't angry at the mention of my parents, he sat up in his chair, fidgety with the energy of validation. He pulled out another cigarette and continued. "Well, some of what we've figured out is true from other religions. You really do get to see your dead relatives, the people you care about again, man. We really do have a soul, something that animates our bodies and leaves when we close our eyes. One of the things that's always bothered me so much about Christianity is that it claims God created heaven and Earth...but what about all that other crap? All those other stars? They make it sound as if there aren't a trillion other stars out there that he governs, but with this theory, it's simple. He did create all those other stars because they're really the same star."

He blew smoke circles toward the stars, mocking them with an *I've figured you out* look in his eyes.

"I believe in God, but not free will," I said. "I believe that every action, every thought that every person ever does or has, has been pre-figured, decided, written by God. Must have taken millions of years to write all that, but it's all pre-programmed. God did give us the ability to believe in free will though, don't you think? Like, he wrote that we'd be sitting here having this conversation, wrote that you'd think up this new theory."

"Yeah, man. You can believe anything you want to believe, I'm not sure how free will and predetermination figure into my Same-Star theory here. What I do believe is, if he wrote it all, he did take the time to make each life we experience around each star slightly different."

Despite everything I'd known about Scuzzy—his disdain of structure, his outward sketchiness—it was a romantically optimistic outlook on everything. Somehow he'd managed to create a philosophy which empowered God, eliminated death, and made it so we never really lose the people we care about.

His carefree demeanor became a little clearer.

"You hungry?" I asked.

"Nah, man, but I could take a walk. Stretch my legs a little." He folded up his chair, picked up the hookah, and placed both just inside the front door.

We started walking. Two more cigarettes. Twice the smoke blown toward the stars.

I could have said anything in the world to him and he wouldn't have judged me. Asked him for any favor and he would have helped me.

"I've got a little theory myself." I said. "It's not as large-scale as yours, but I believe in it."

"Shoot, man."

"I believe there are times you can archive in your life, things you can put a little tag on and they go on a list of stuff you want to review with God when you die. If you die. So you can see what would have happened if you went left instead of right. Or find out what someone was really thinking at an important moment when you were talking to them. Shit like that."

"Like an exit consultation on life?"

"Yeah, sort of. Like when you die and go to heaven—if you go to heaven—God smiles, spreads his arms and says, *So what do you want to know?* And then you finally get some answers."

He considered it. Flicked his cigarette to the base of a tree that never blooms, but isn't dead—doesn't rot.

"And if there is a heaven and we go there, everyone appears exactly how you want to see them, how you remember them. The same man when looked at, at the same exact time by his mother and his son, is seen as both a child in the eyes of one and an adult in the eyes of the other."

"I'm going to hashtag this to my list," he said. "If we have a list, I want this moment added to mine so that on that exit consultation, God can tell me if we're even close on any of this. Another thing that always bothered me about Christianity is the idea of time in heaven. If heaven is timeless, then we should all already be there."

He spit that smoky saliva into the street, again, as we crossed it. "But we're not, Matt. We're here. We're real and we feel pain. You of all people know that."

I thought about the red bricks hidden beneath the street. Something that had been there all along, hidden just out of sight, like the answers we were searching for.

He dropped me off at Midnight Breakfast with a handshake. He used the handshake to pull me into a hug. And during the hug, he must have lifted the trillion dollar bill from my pocket. I never saw it again.

THE DINING HALL WAS PACKED. I entered Skillet, grabbed a tray, filled it with powdered eggs, questionable sausage, and diced peaches, and sat down at a crowded table alone. The peaches made me think of my mom. She used to send me to grammar school with peaches in a tin can, the kind that had a pull-tab on top that the teacher always had to help me open before snack time. I can remember eating them in the classroom at my desk as early as kindergarten.

Through the glass ceiling, I looked up at the soft light from that dark, distant sky and tried to picture her face. It was getting harder and harder. I sat there a long time, eating peaches and wondering if the sweaty handprints on the clear ceiling were from kids trying to get in or kids trying to get out.

I Realized

What We Wish For

SOMETIME DURING JUNIOR YEAR, I decided to look for a job because there didn't seem to be anything else to do. I realized that work for the sake of work can help the despondent find meaning again. My friends were happy when I told them I was going to be doing something constructive with my time. There was so much construction going on around The University, and I began to want to be a part of it, putting new things where old things once stood. For a while, I thought it might be fun to help build something, to leave a handprint somewhere in wet concrete.

AN OLD MAN WAS TORMENTING birds down at Passion Pond in the middle of campus. He had hooked a hunk of bread on the end of a fishing line and cast it close enough to the water to lure the fowl out. They shook themselves dry, casting grimy water droplets that caught the sun, a tiny rainbow in each wet bead that fell from their feathers to the grass. The man began reeling in the bread, and the birds waddled after it until they got too close to the old man and stopped, ten feet away, as if hindered by an unseen barrier. They looked hungry, disappointed. All hope is dashed at some point.

It didn't take long to realize that I wasn't qualified for anything, that college may not have been preparing me for whatever it should have been preparing me for.

LIKE EVERY OTHER COLLEGE student, I got a job in the service industry. There was a little French café next to the student center bus stop where some smart businessmen made a killing charging caffeine-addicted college students four dollars for cups of mediocre coffee. The place had a good reputation because they had plenty of tables close to outlets and they kept the room freezing cold so the coffee tasted better. The place became a haven for all-nighters and aspiring writers, a popular meeting spot for group projects.

Like anyone else who has ever worked in the service industry, I realized right away that every person is a fuck. I had been working there just over a month when a woman came up to me and said, "You know, you should smile while you work. It's more pleasant."

When I told her that both of my parents had been dead since I was fourteen, she shut her mouth. At least to my face, that was the end of it. But she complained to my manager, anyway—got me fired because she was bored with her life and figured that hurting someone else might give her some excitement. From there I found a flower shop and worked for a florist. That job was my life for a while. The opportunity to be creative meant the world to me. It was like painting with flowers and it was the first thing I loved doing in years. But I couldn't escape death there either. Flowers passed away all around me every day and I couldn't handle it.

I was way too fragile to work when I didn't need the money.

THERE'S NOTHING FUNNY about a shooting star. While you're making a wish on that shooting star, it's dying—dying a slow, glorious death. They say you should never tell anyone what you wish for, because then your wish won't come true. But that isn't true. I have made plenty of wishes that came true even though I'd told people about them. When I was a little boy, I realized that the real secret to wishing on a star is to not look at it twice. The real secret is to make your wish and get the hell out. Look down and don't look back up at that same star, no matter how bad you want to.

One time, I went to the beach alone at night and stood with my ankles in the water, getting dizzy each time a wave pulled out and loosened the sand beneath my feet. I saw it slicing across my peripheral vision. Looking up at the dying star, I made my wish and lowered my eyes to the water.

What did I wish for? I wished for the same thing we all wish for—what every person with a regret wishes for. And then I stared out across the Atlantic Ocean and wondered if somewhere off the coast of England, there was a boy with his feet in the water doing the exact same thing as me.

MY ONLY FRIEND FROM across the sea was my buddy Sash. By the spring semester of our freshman year, fraternities had heard about the two of us. Word had spread of two financially endowed freshmen running around enjoying life, and they all set their minds to scheming up ways to draw us in.

Sash was from Dubai. We'd been floor mates that first year, formed an unlikely pair. A Middle Eastern young man with the money of a foreign prince, and a middleclass American white boy who didn't want the money he had. We tore shit up, the two of us, pretending that we were interested in every fraternity. We went to all their interest events for free, ate the food their recruiting chairmen put out for free, got invited to mixers that only brothers were supposed to go to and got the girls and the drinks for free.

Many of them were noble. I saw teenagers turn down ragers so that they could wake up at 5:00AM to help set up cancer walk-a-thons. I didn't have that openness in my heart. Knew I lacked some of the finer elements of Greek life and could never handle the rules and by-laws that governed them. The only thing I could offer a brotherhood was unaccountability. And that was fine with me. I realized that real freedom sometimes means being alone.

I WAS ALONE IN MY ROOM with this kid Riley, after winter break senior year, planning out our last spring break. The pressure of the real world was starting to get to us even though we had not reached it yet. It loomed with all the impending doom of a super storm, ready to change things, to erase the way we lived and the way we loved.

We were always planning things, Riley and me. Like the time we planned to rent a car and drive across country, all the way to Cali, where we were three hours younger, three hours further from the real world. Using a fake ID, I'd rented a powder-blue Ferrari for a month, packed the trunk full of alcohol and clothes and other supplies. Riley's mom had given us a hard time as we were leaving. She was paranoid that he was going to do porn once we got out there.

"I know what it's like," she said. "Sleeping with anyone and everyone. Next thing you know, I'll get a call from someone who's seen you—all of you—online."

"Mom, it's not like that. We're just going to stick our feet in the Pacific, smoke a little weed, unwind."

Las Vegas was as far as we got, though. It was a tale of two trips for us. Riley went broke in half a day and spent the rest of the month working a minimum wage job cleaning toilets at the Bellagio. I, on the other hand, couldn't lose. It was as if I were being repaid for a lifetime of shit luck. Riley wouldn't take any of the money I offered him.

"There's a fine line between friendship and charity," he said.

"Just take the fucking money."

"No way. I'd rather clean toilets."

Riley was cool like that. It didn't take me long to realize that he was my friend, not my groupie.

One spring break we went to New Orleans for Mardi Gras. When our friends realized where we were going, two dozen people tagged along, and I ended up paying for all their rooms. A day after we got down there, on an impulse, Riley and I broke away from the group and made our way over to the St. Louis Cathedral, which overlooks Jackson Square. We spent most of our time there in the Louisiana State Museum, looking at exhibits of what Katrina had done. We met a fortune teller in the shadow of the statue of Andrew Jackson riding his horse.

"How much?" I asked.

"Ten dollars."

I handed her the money, grabbed Riley by the wrist, and handed her his hand. The woman rolled it over, pressed his fingers flat, leaned her face in close, and began running her fingertips over the lines of his palm.

"Stay still," she said.

"But it tickles."

After a moment, she began muttering to herself and then offered, "These three lines symbolize three important decisions you will have to make in your life. Two of them cross again later, so never take too long to make up your mind. Follow your heart."

She dropped his palm and took a step back.

"That's it?" Riley asked.

The woman shrugged her shoulders.

"Aren't you gonna tell me my future or some shit? How many kids I'll have? When I'm gonna die?"

The woman pressed her hand over the money in her pocket, protecting it. I grabbed Riley by the arm and led him away. I didn't want him to offend her, but I was afraid that if we stayed any longer, Riley would demand I get my palm read, too.

For our last spring break we wanted to go back-packing through Europe for those nine days, to see where most of the world's history had taken place, but nothing ever came of it. We spent too long planning, never even got as far as booking the plane tickets. We ran out of time. We all run out of it eventually.

BUT BEFORE WE RAN OUT of time…before the real world caught up to us…I realized that it feels just as good to fall out of love with someone as it does to fall into it.

"Maybe things will be different someday," Courtney said.

It always bothered me how people could go from such a high level of intimacy with someone one moment to wanting to hurt them as bad as they could the next.

"I will always be in your corner," I told her. It would have been senseless burning a bridge that may someday lead back to somewhere I already know is beautiful.

It all comes back to construction. Building new things where old ones once stood, because all bridges get worn and brittle over time.

After the breakup, I was alone and free again. Out from under the thumb of love, I took to driving without a destination. Behind the wheel of my old Ford Taurus—a heavy silver tank on wheels—I began thinking of a girl I used to know.

Her name was Angelica, the most popular girl in my high school class. In fifth grade—our moms got to talking at a school carnival, and when we got home, my mom told me that Angelica had a crush on me.

God only knows how much different my life would have been if I had asked her out, but I was an insecure ten-year-old boy. If I had asked her to be my girlfriend at that age, she may have been my wife.

Ten years old is too young for anyone to have a significant other. Our innocence together would have protected us from the corruption of growing up. We would have been together just before social pressure called for us to be interested in one another. The liking would have been genuine.

Instead, I never talked to her. I stayed away from her, because she had a reputation for being aggressive, and most boys were afraid of her. In middle school, she was violent toward boys. By high school, she was dating a different upperclassman every week.

I saw her at a Thanksgiving weekend party—the secret first high school reunion—the first time everyone was back in our hometown since we had all splintered off across the country to different colleges.

"Matthew?" I heard her before I saw her. Her voice was familiar, even though we'd never been that close. Gripping my elbow, she spun me sideways. "Matthew Rose, how have you been?"

She wore a black leather jacket and tight skinny-jeans. She had heavy makeup caked on her face, but even in the poor lighting of a stranger's dingy basement, I could see the past bright in her eyes. The baby-roundness in her cheeks was still there even though she'd been so grown up for so long.

"Angelica, it's great to see you."

I meant it. Seeing her made me feel younger. I was still intimidated by her—a ten-year-old boy with an unwritten future.

"What are you doing with yourself these days? Where are you going to college? What are you studying?"

Through the meaningless cookie-cutter conversation you have with every person you see from high school while you're in college, there was personal tension between us. The resentment I saw in her was real, so hot that I could feel my cheeks burn.

Why the fuck didn't you ask me out? You were my first crush, and life could have been that simple, was what she really wanted to say.

Because I was scared and stupid and a fucking idiot.

This is not how things were supposed to be. I know you knew I liked you.

I'm so sorry, I wanted to tell her. *Not asking you to be my girlfriend is one of the biggest regrets I have.*

But none of that would have done either of us any good. It was eight years too late. She offered me a cigarette. I took it, and we spent the next few minutes inhaling nicotine a few feet apart, wishing we could do things over.

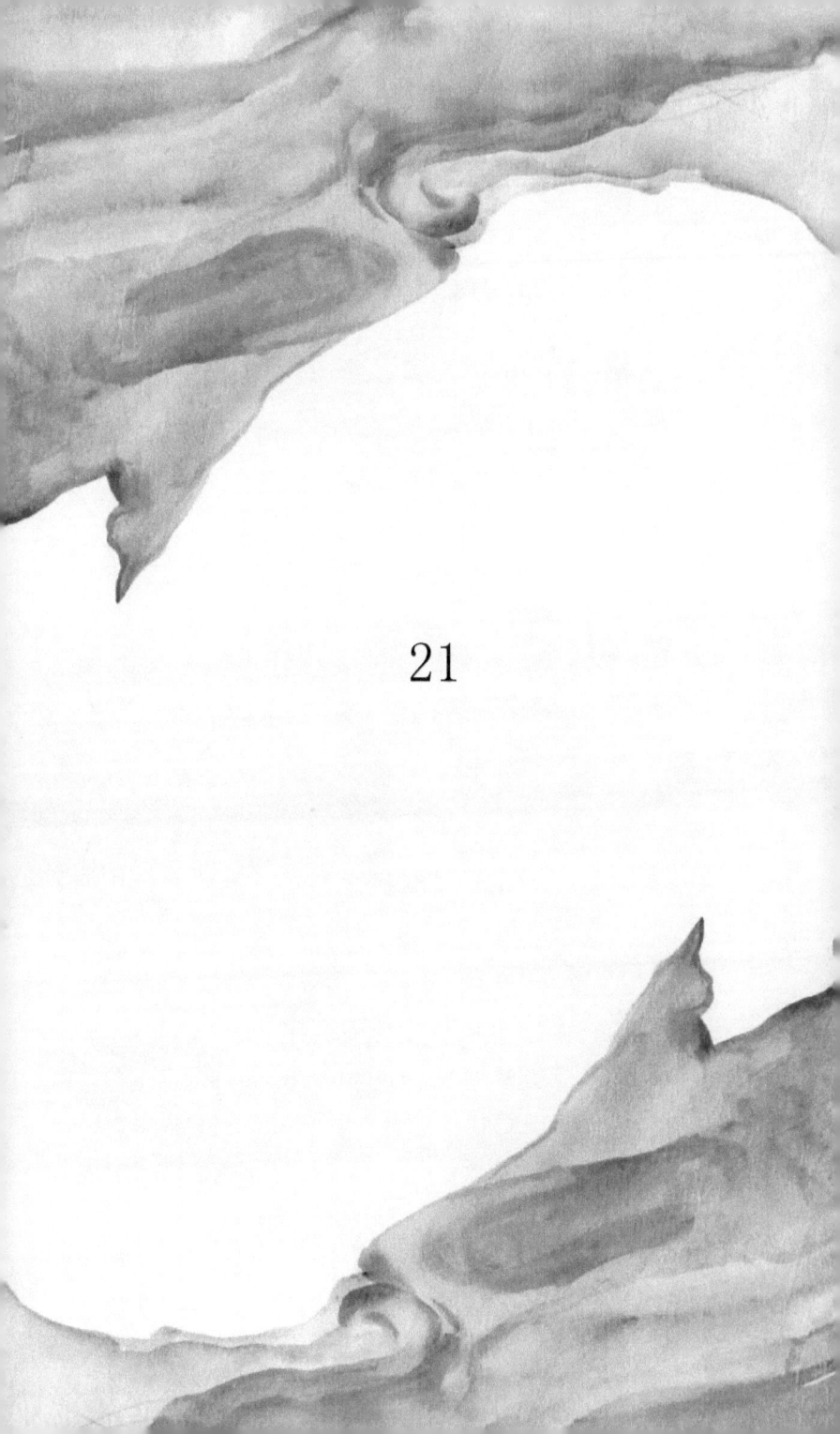

21

I T WAS A TRADITION THAT started a long time ago. Way back before anyone noticed, roommates began cutting their "U" in half and signing them with their floor mates. By then they were sunworn and faded. So tired out by life that they no longer shined.

IT WAS A TRADITION THAT started on my birthday.

The first one after my mother died. Leaving me alone to wonder what it means to carry parts of people with you into the future.

This and my name, was what they left me.

Not the money.

IN THE WINDOW OF EVERY dorm room, The University taped a cardboard "U."

"Hurry up and sign it, Dubian," I told Sash.

"Some things take time, Matty boy," he said.

He'd been staring at my half for twenty minutes, and I was tired of waiting.

"I want to get this right. In fifty years, this is how you will remember me. By the few words I write here on this shit piece of cardboard."

Inspiration struck him then. He put his pen down as I wondered if he could really be right. Did all things boil down to a few words in the end?

"Boom! There you go." He handed my half a "U" back to me. I handed his back to him, and walked out of the room. Things like that need to be read in privacy. If I cried in front of him, he'd never have seen me the same way again.

I NEVER ASKED THEM TO COME. But they offered to go with me, and I was touched.

"You're not going to be alone on your birthday. Not this year, buddy," Sash said.

The four of us were on a train.

"Drink this." Skeeter handed me a Poland Spring bottle concealed in a paper bag. The liquid inside was brown and I gave him a look.

"Just drink it," he said. "It will make you feel better. I promise."

I took a sip, coughed through the burn. Riley was flipping through an old newspaper that had been orphaned by a commuter. "Don't see nothin' in here about no pity party."

"Shut the fuck up," Sash told him. And he did.

There wasn't anyone else in the car with us. It was close to midnight and we were on the last ride away from The University.

"I still can't believe this is where you disappear to on your birthday every year," Skeeter said. "I would have gone with you last year and the year before that if I'd known."

I reminded him that I liked to go alone.

"Bet you twenty bucks the place is closed," Riley said.

"No shit, Sherlock. Of course it's gonna be closed," Sash said.

"Well someone make a bet with me then, I could really use the money."

So I told Riley I'd take the bet. We shook on it and he closed his eyes, went from sulking to satisfied real fast.

Sash took the newspaper off his lap, rolled it up, and looked at me through it like he was using a telescope. I remembered the last time I almost cried in front of him, two years ago, when we were freshmen. There would be nowhere to run, this time. They were going to see me cry when we got to the cemetery.

———

RILEY STUCK HIS HAND OUT, and I handed him a twenty-dollar-bill.

"First round tomorrow night's on me," he said.

I called him a prince as they pushed me up over the wall.

When we were all on the other side, I led the way toward my parents.

"You okay, buddy?" Sash laid a flat hand across my shoulder, and squeezed.

I kept my eyes straight ahead. Scanned row after row until I found it. *ROSE* inscribed on a headstone that I had kissed many times.

They all went quiet, waited for me to say something. It was the longest I'd ever heard Riley go without talking.

The sound of Sash's lighter sparking echoed across the graveyard. We sat there, cross-legged like little kids, smoking his hashish under the black, cloudy sky.

"Happy birthday, buddy," he said to me.

It was the best birthday I'd had in a long, long time.

WE CAUGHT THE FIRST train back to The University in the morning. A 5AM ride riddled with zombies sleepwalking their way to work. Skeeter and Riley fell asleep as soon as we started moving, they snored loud and I kicked their feet now and then to keep them quiet. Sash and I were wide awake. The kid was like an owl, sitting across from me with big eyes, his lanky legs mingling with mine in the shared footspace.

"There's something different about you," he said.

It was the moment I'd been dreading. Where part of Sash's respect for me would be replaced by pity.

"You look happy."

I didn't know what to say. I felt naked in front of him, and my face got hot.

"I'm gonna crash when I get back to my apartment. Sleep it off and I'll be good for tonight," I told him.

You only turn twenty-one once, and the bar crawl the guys had planned for me would make it a great night to forget.

That sounded good to me. But it left me with more unanswerable questions.

Is it better to forget or to remember?

Is it sadder to let tradition die or to do the same thing over and over again as it tears you apart?

"YOU SOUND SURPRISED, MATTHEW."

"I'm always surprised when a man comes back from the dead."

"I'm not dead, I'm missing."

"No, you're dead. I'm not falling for it again."

"I don't feel dead."

"Well, Mom and I buried you years ago."

"You haven't buried anything."

"I miss you."

"Matthew, I'm missing. Of course you miss me."

"Do you really mean it?"

"That I'm not dead?"

"Yes."

"Yes."

"So it is true then…"

"What's true, Matthew?"

"That there is a heaven."

"Heaven…"

"What are you looking at?"

"Your mother says hi, son."

"Please don't. I'll start to cry again. I know you're not real."

"I'm not—"

"Dead, I know."

"As long as you know."

"We buried you. And then I…"

"Please don't or you'll make me cry, too."

"Ghosts can't cry, can they?"

"I told you I'm not dead. So how can I be a ghost?"

"She and I buried you and after that I buried…"

"Mine was an empty coffin."

"Hers wasn't."

"I know, son."

"She looked beautiful."

"I know, I was there. She still is beautiful."

"I knew you were there with us, with me. I could feel you. I had a hard time feeling you before I buried—"

"That's because you needed me then."

"I still need you, I will always need you. But you're missing."

"Yes, missing."

"She really was beautiful."

"Matthew…"

"Tell her I miss her, too."

I WOKE UP FROM MY NAP to banging on my door.

"Wake the fuck up! Make me break this door down, and I swear I will! I'll drag your ass out by the dick if I have to, buddy!"

Sash and Skeeter and Riley were ready to go. They all wore button downs, dress pants, dress shoes. Riley had even slicked his hair back.

"You do that for me?" I asked him.

He smiled at me the way he did when I had made the bet with him. He could be a real charmer when he was in a good mood. I walked down the hallway to my bedroom to get ready. Sash followed me and sat down on my bed.

"That shirt's wrinkly," he said.

"It's clean though, Dubian."

He went to my closet, and pulled the ironing board out. By the time he was finished and I washed my hair, I was looking almost as good as Riley.

"Matty Rose finally turns twenty-one." Skeeter jabbed my shoulder when I walked into the living room. We did a Jägerbomb and by then I was starting to feel real good.

"Should I bring a jacket?" I asked as we got ready to leave.

"Is it a good jacket?" Skeeter asked me.

"It's my favorite jacket."

"Definitely leave it then."

We made our way down Weston Ave to Corner Pub. There was no bouncer, they didn't even bother to card us. Inside, the lights were yellow, the wood paneling smelt like wet newspaper, and the only other patrons were a couple of bikers in denim jeans and matching leather jackets. A middle-aged woman behind the bar asked us what we wanted.

"Two four-horsemen," Skeeter said.

"I'm buying his first drink." Riley laid the twenty I'd given him yesterday down on the bar.

"He's already had two drinks. The Jägerbomb counts as two."

"Like hell it does."

"He drank them. They count," Sash said.

The bartender poured four shots, took the twenty, didn't return with any change.

We all took one and raised it.

"It's about fucking time we're celebrating things right," Riley toasted.

I recognized the burn from the train ride.

"What's in it?" I asked Skeeter.

"Wiki it later," he told me.

"That's three drinks." Riley held up three fingers and wiggled them, "I'll keep count for you."

Sash handed me a beer. "Let's get out of here. That better be finished by the time we get to the next bar."

Riley whispered, "Four," as we headed for the door.

"GIVE HIM A BLOWJOB," Sash told the bartender.

"Good call," Skeeter laughed.

The bartender poured a coffee-looking shot, capped it off with some whipped cream. I went to pick it up and Sash grabbed my wrist. "No hands."

I bent my face down to the bar, and sucked it down.

"Five," Riley said.

Steel Tracks is a cool bar. It's dark inside, the only light comes from the thirty TVs that ring the walls. Skeeter took my ID, got me a free t-shirt and cheap bottle of champagne because it was my birthday. He poured himself, Sash, and Riley a sip each in a plastic cup and handed me the rest of the bottle.

"We'll count that as three drinks once you kill it," Riley said.

"To feeling good," Skeeter toasted.

They took their sips, I chugged the bottle. It tasted like piss and made me gag. Sash pulled the t-shirt over my head, and we all threw our arms around each other for a selfie.

"That's eight," Riley told me. "How ya feeling?"

"Too good, I think."

Sash handed me another beer and led us toward the door.

I really was feeling good. Dizzy and numb.

"I miss Scuzzy," I said.

"Where is he?" Sash asked. "How haven't I ever met that kid?"

"He's home for the weekend."

"He's really missing your birthday?" Riley asked. He knew Scuzzy well, knew there had to be a good reason for him to not be here.

"It's his mother's birthday this weekend, too," I told him.

"Ah, family comes first." As soon as the words left Riley's mouth he realized he'd made a mistake.

I changed the subject by crushing my beer can, tossed it into the gutter.

"Nine," Riley said.

Sash flashed his VIP card at the bouncer of Nightclub and led us to his favorite spot, on the back wall.

"Four Fireball shots, two shots of Patrón, and one rum and coke," he ordered. "Don't worry, Matty boy, they're not all for you. We'll do the Fireballs with you. You're taking both Patrón though and the rum and coke is to sip between shots. I'd swallow some ice, if I were you."

We each took a shot, raised it to each other.

"To being alive," Sash toasted.

"Ten," Riley said.

"Eleven," Riley said.

"Twelve," Riley said.

I was doing real good until my fourteenth drink. Then it was like I got punched in the face. The last thing I remember is Sash's eyes, green like saltwater rust. I thought back to what he'd written for me years ago at the end of freshman year.

"You were right," I said to him.

And the rest of the night was forgotten.

———

NOTHING AT THE CORNER of *Memory* & *What-TheFuckHappened.*

My eyes hurt and I was weak—real weak.

"Ughhhh…"

Out of nowhere Sash was at my side.

"Boom! He lives."

I tried to talk but coughed instead. Blood came out of me and freckled my white pillowcase.

"Not for long," I said.

"Oh, buddy, that's bad."

"What's bad?" Skeeter and Riley walked in. Even then, they look like aces. Their hair was a mess and their eyes were bloodshot, but there wasn't a wrinkle in either one of their shirts.

Sash pointed at my pillow.

"Shit, we gotta take him to the hospital," Skeeter said.

"I'm fine."

Sash put his hand on my forehead. "No fever. No fever, no hospital."

"He needs help." Skeeter looked pale and this worried me.

"I'm really fine."

Riley sat on the foot of my bed, smiled at me and I wondered what was so funny.

"What the fuck could be wrong with him?" Sash yelled.

"I don't know, asshole, but he's spitting up blood for a reason."

"I sat here all night. He's still breathing. He's fine."

"Something's wrong with him."

"Nothing's wrong with him." Sash stood up, looked down at me, "Snap the fuck out of it."

He walked out. We heard the living room window open and a second later, the flick of a lighter.

Skeeter looked down at me then.

"Really, I'm fine."

"Do what you want. But don't listen to Sash."

He looked at Riley and now they both laughed.

"What's so funny?" I asked.

"You don't remember, do you?" Riley asked.

"Let's just say you and Riley are much better friends than you were yesterday," Skeeter said.

I sat up, reached for one of the water bottles I had next to the bed and chugged the whole thing.

"You were all over the place at Nightclub. Knocking drinks out of people's hands, almost getting into fights. We got you back to your place and you started ripping at your eyes trying to take your contacts out. Skeeter held you down while I pulled them out. Then you threw up all over yourself."

"Shit," I said.

"It gets better," Skeeter laughed.

"Well I took your shirt off, and your pants off. And you said you really needed to pee. So I walked you to the bathroom and figured I could at least let you do that on your own. So I'm right outside the door waiting and I don't hear piss hitting water—"

"—So he opens the door and there you are naked on the floor, pissing with your dick in your hand." Skeeter finished the story and laughed so hard he forgot I'd been spitting up blood.

Riley blushed. "You're probably fine. You threw up so much that your stomach acid probably burnt up your esophagus. Just don't suck any dick because your throat's gonna be pretty raw for a few days, I'll bet."

"Do what you want," Skeeter said, then left the room to go argue with Sash some more.

"Did all that really happen, or are you just fucking with me?"

Riley patted my leg, looked at me the way I imagine a brother would. "It's okay if you don't remember," he said. "I'll never let you forget it."

I didn't care that he saw me cry.

ALONE, BACK IN MY DORM ROOM, I looked down at my half of the "U."

For years, roommates had been cutting them in half.

Carrying pieces of each other into the future.

I read what the people of House 24 had written for me to remember them by, wondered if things would ever get better.

```
Matty boy,
You can try as hard as you want, but
you'll never be completely alone.
Boom!
-Dubian
```

And he was right.

You can do everything possible to cut yourself off from the world—put up walls, reinforce them with concrete and steel—but like it or not, good people are still going to find you.

They will fight for you.

Whether you want them to or not.

And they will always find a way to break through.

Counting Heartbeats

I HELD HIS HAND, AND HE HELD mine tight. We were walking across a blacktop and he was barefoot.

"Where did you come from?" I asked.

He shrugged his shoulders, and leaned his head against my hip. "Can we stop?"

We sat down in the tall grass just before the road. The car was up ahead, a hundred yards out of reach. The boy pulled up gobs of earth and packed it between his toes.

"Can you carry me?" he asked.

And when I lifted him, green blades rained down from his feet.

"How old are you?"

"Five and three quarters," he said.

"Are you hungry?"

He licked his lips and his grip tightened across my shoulder blades. With one hand, I opened the door, set him down in the passenger seat of the Mustang.

"I'm Luke," he said.

———

EARLIER, A HOTDOG VENDER had sold me pills that tasted like candy. He worked a street corner near The University, peddling unmarked prescription bottles to students and reprobates.

I bought two, was on my way out of town with Sash in his new red Mustang convertible. We were headed to see this girl he used to know, and when my buddy Scuzzy found out we were leaving school, he invited himself along for the ride.

"Shit man, where'd you get this car? This shit is sick."

"It's Sash's toy of the month," I told Scuzzy, punching Sash's arm.

It was that time of year when the weather was just starting to warm. Sash flicked a switch and the roof retracted, revealing a cloudless blue sky that could make a small boy cry. A few minutes later, we were flying down the interstate, listening to the wind and sipping Lokos as we drove because we needed the caffeine.

In the back, Scuzzy popped the top on one of the bottles and swallowed a couple of the pills.

"Where'd you get these?" he asked.

"Does he ever shut up?" Sash shot me a look out of the corner of his eye.

This was business for him, and it takes patience to handle Scuzzy. I buffered by talking about the girl we were on our way to see.

"Do you love her?" I asked. Sash shook his head, but his white knuckles on the steering wheel betrayed him.

Just then Scuzzy leaned up real close to my ear from the behind and whispered, "What's her name?"

"Her name is Amy. And if you don't put your fucking seatbelt on, I'm going to crash this car right now and wreck you," Sash said.

I heard a seatbelt click, and we all went back to looking at how the crowded buildings of the city gave way to the more open landscape of the suburbs.

The trees were just starting to come back from the dead. Branches, all over, burst to life with color that screamed, *I'm alive!*

Soon, Sash slowed the car down in front of a faded-brown ranch house, and a girl sprung from the porch. Without putting the car in park, Sash hopped out over the side door and ran to her.

"It's been so long," I heard her say.

But I couldn't make out what he said back.

"Hey, we're still moving, man!" Scuzzy jumped out of the car and ran alongside it. "Don't worry, man. I'll stop it."

With both hands pressed against the hood of the car, he backpedaled and groaned, "Stay, you fucking horse. Stay, or I'll break you."

"Get back in here before you get killed!"

"No way, man. Gotta stop this 'Stang."

I imagined what the sounds would be like if I were still in the car while it ran him over. I scrambled behind the wheel and slammed hard on the breaks. The car stopped and Scuzzy hopped into the passenger seat, wiping his hands on his jeans, looking real satisfied.

"You're welcome," he said. Then he pointed toward the sky and yelled, "Hey, look! Geese!"

Up above, several birds were making their way back north. Clouds dotted the atmosphere now, puffs a pure white that you almost never see in the world anymore.

We followed them in the car, the birds and the clouds. Doing the best we could from below to not lose the beauty we'd found up above.

"Fuckers are getting away," Scuzzy said. "Maybe you should let me drive, man."

"No way."

"Then go faster," he urged. "We can't lose them."

I can't say why it seemed so important that we keep them in sight. It felt as if we were a step behind something significant. As we drove on, they got smaller and smaller, like balloons floating away from the outstretched hand of a child.

We lost them.

"I'm so sorry," I said.

And Scuzzy fell quiet. He fell quiet until his eyes burst open like the trees coming back to life. "Nah, it's no big deal, man. There will always be more birds."

He yanked on the emergency break. "Let's get out and wait for more."

Before I knew it, he was out of the car and racing through a school playground. By the time I parked and caught up to him, he was laying on his back in the middle of a soccer field, hands folded across his chest. I lay down beside him, cupped my hands behind my head, and there we were. The two of us, children again, picking out clouds and counting birds that flew by.

He passed me one of the pill bottles and we watched the sunset like this. From blue to orange and from orange to purple, it all looked like a painting. I'd watched and painted so many sunsets, but none stood out quite like this.

Scuzzy slid his hand under his shirt and began counting, "One…two…three…four…"

"What are you doing?"

"Heartbeats, man. Counting heartbeats."

This, to me, seemed beautiful.

"I wonder how Sash is doing," I said.

"Oh, I think he's doing alright," he turned and winked at me. "Not as good as us, but I'm sure he's doing OK."

When the bottle was empty, I stood up, dropped it to the ground, and crushed it with the heel of my foot. A cracking sound echoed across the field, the sound of bones breaking.

"Shit, fucking bugs!" Scuzzy jumped up, began scratching his arms hard with his fingernails. "They're all over me, man! Help! Get 'em off!"

Painful, red lines rose on his forearms.

"Stop, you're gonna draw blood."

"Please, man! The bugs are crawling all over me!"

"I think you're seeing things," I said, grabbing his arms, trying to hold him still.

"Tripping over bugs? No way, man. They're real and they're everywhere."

I wrapped my arms around him, tackled him to the ground as gentle as I could.

"Hey, what gives? Get off me, man."

With my knees pinning his wrists, I sat on his chest to keep him from hurting himself. He only struggled for a few minutes. Soon, he forgot about the bugs he was seeing. His breathing steadied and it wasn't long before he was asleep.

Once I was sure he wasn't faking, I rolled off and closed my eyes beside him.

A LONG WHILE LATER, I woke up and he was gone.

Next to me, where Scuzzy had been, I found the other bottle of pills weighing down a note scrawled on the back of a drugstore receipt.

Matt, gone to look for more birds.
You keep these, you need them more
than I do, man.

I picked up the bottle, stood up too fast and fell
back down.

Movement on the playground caught my eye. A
lone swing rocking back and forth. On its seat sat a
barefoot boy who stared back at me.

"You okay?" I called out to him, expecting him to
run as I approached, but he stayed put, his knuckles white
and his fingertips black underneath at the nails.

I took the seat next to him, and his legs started
pumping. I swung mine, too, getting high with him.

And I swear, I almost saw him smile.

"DID YOU RUN AWAY?" I asked Luke. "I should
probably take you home."

He picked his nose and wiped it on the leather
seat.

The rain came out of nowhere, started slow at
first—tiny droplets of water that speckled the windshield
and looked like tears just before the wipers smeared them.
All at once I got thirsty. Instead of pulling over to put the

roof of the Mustang back up, I opened my mouth and looked toward the starless sky.

Luke copied me, and this was how we drove. Mouths open to the rain, my eyes straining for the road. That's when the nausea set in and my mouth tasted like dry fire. I pulled into the next parking lot I saw, and we walked into a bar called *John's*.

"Let's get you some food," I said to Luke.

Inside, the lights were dim and the people were old. The faded gray walls were spackled white where holes had been. On every table sat the same fake wax candles, the kinds with the little switches underneath and the batteries that seem to last forever.

"What'll it be?" the bartender asked me, then he eyeballed Luke.

The kid stared back at him, sniffled, and wiped his nose with the back of his hand.

"Can I get a water, a ginger ale, and two baskets of chicken fingers?" I asked.

A pregnant woman looked up from her drink at us as if we were something strange to see, then went back to tracing her fingers in the sad water rings on the bar. Everyone else in the place looked lost in their own misery.

"Eighteen-fifty, son. Chicken will be right out," the bartender said as he placed the drinks down in front of Luke and I.

My wallet was home on my dresser. Sometimes I do that—leave my money behind so that I can escape it—or at least forget it long enough so that I don't feel like myself anymore. I'd taken only what it would cost for the pills, because that was all I needed.

"Can you get that," I said to the man sitting next to me. "I've got two pills worth $10 each for you if you do."

The man lifted his head so that I could see his boney, drawn cheeks, straight, dark-brown hair, and bloodshot eyes. "Me?" he said, a smile spreading across his face.

"You going to pay for the kid or not?" the bartender asked.

"Oh, yes. Yes, of course."

"Thanks. What's your name?" I asked the man.

"Mark. Where are the pills?"

I slid two across the bar to him. Mark picked them up and examined them, holding them close to one of the fake candles.

"What are they?"

I pretended not to hear him as I guzzled down the ginger ale. It did little to help settle my stomach. My body had just about had enough. Inside, everything felt like gears grinding, steel melting, concrete crumbling. Like things were all out of place but somehow still struggling to function.

Mark slid a twenty-dollar-bill across the bar, picking up our bill. Luke guzzled his water through a straw, picked up the glass and chewed on the ice.

I imagined his baby teeth breaking.

"Don't chew ice," I told him.

He leaned his head into my arm. The pill bottle rattled in my pocket and I felt disgusted with myself.

"I'll pretend I didn't just see any of that for a ten dollar tip," the bartender said.

There wasn't much of a choice for me. I hate when people do that. I'd probably have offered him one anyway at some point, but I hate when people take something from you before you have a chance to give it to them. He smiled, thinking he'd gotten one over on me.

"Give me another ginger ale, and I'll give you one."

It was like we were at a flea market, bargaining, negotiating our way to the things we all wanted.

He set down another sparkling glass and said, "I'll keep them coming."

As Luke busied himself stealing onion rings off the plate of the woman next to him, I thought of Scuzzy. If anyone could find birds at night time, it would be him.

Our food came and we gobbled it up. It had been twelve hours since my last meal. It was too little too late though. Nausea gave way to dizziness. I staggered out the door like a wounded soldier, must have fallen and rolled over onto my back.

Luke looked over me, his ketchup-stained, wide-eyed face calm as can be, "You'll be okay," he said.

THE NEXT THING I KNEW, we were chasing butterflies down the middle of a dead end street. They were colorful and wonderful, but they were not birds. Still though, they were flying, and I thought that this might be good enough.

At the end of the cul-de-sac there was a lone lamp flickering on and off, electrifying the rain around it, turning water into sparks. The butterflies hovered around the light, circling the lamp like planets orbiting the sun, until one of them strayed from the group and whispered my name.

"Matthew," the butterfly said, and I was sure then that I was tripping.

"They're so pretty," Luke said.

We were getting poured on. Our clothes grew heavy but my heart beat out hope in my chest.

"What did you just say?"

"They're so pretty," he repeated.

"You see them, too?"

"Uh, huh."

"You see the butterflies?"

"Yes," he said, "I see them."

"Even the pink ones?" I asked him, it seemed important that he saw the pink ones.

"The pink ones and the purple ones and the red ones and the orange ones."

"And the blue ones?" I needed to be sure he really saw them.

"Blue and green and yellow…"

Together we followed them. They fell into a V-formation, as geese do to cut the wind, and the same fear that I was a step behind something significant returned. Only this time, I was determined to figure out what it was and hold onto it. They led us away from the dead end road as if that had been their plan all along. It was only once we were out in the middle of a crossroad, with an important decision to make, that they stopped.

"Which way should we go?" I asked Luke. He looked at the butterflies for answers. They flew left.

"Home is this way," Luke said.

He turned right and I followed. I would not argue with him. The butterflies floated in midair, hung still hoping to trance me. I blinked and they became part of the rain.

Luke led the way.

I was a step behind.

———

WE PASSED A POLICE STATION on the way. It was the early AM and no one seemed to miss him.

Luke looked at me like I might betray him.

"You'll be okay," I told him.

"Can you carry me?" he asked, again.

I scooped him up and he was asleep in my arms thirty seconds later. With nowhere to go, I walked in circles around the block as darkness faded and dawn crept. He was so delicate in my arms, but tough where it mattered, on the inside.

"What's your story?" I whispered to him.

"Where is home?" I asked when he stirred.

Luke wiped his eyes with both hands.

"Here," he said, pointing toward a dilapidated white apartment building.

I set him down and he walked up the front steps. I'd gotten him home, and this, I knew, I could get by on.

"Come see my room," he said.

The door was unlocked. Inside, a half-empty bottle of Cuervo Silver sat on the kitchen counter. From a bedroom down the hall I heard snoring.

"Mommy's sleeping," he said.

He mumbled something, laid down on the couch, was out cold again by the time I put a blanket over him.

I sat on the coffee table, watched him sleep for a few minutes. Air and life pulling in through his nose, his chest rising and falling.

How could I leave him?

His arm fell limp, hanging off the side of the couch. With two fingers I picked it up, tucked his hand under his leg to keep it in place.

And then I went back for it. Put my fingers to the inside of his tiny wrist.

One…two…three…four…

This, I knew, I could get by on, forever.

Acknowledgements

As always, thank you to Kelly Smith for her guidance, advice, and patience, all of which have made it possible for me to go after my dreams. Thank you to John Martinetti of JEM Graphics for his hard work on the website and for always making me laugh. Thank you to David Fulcher of *Samsara Magazine*, Roxana Nastase of *Scarlet Leaf Review*, and the *Five 2 One* staff for first-publishing several of these stories in their fine literary magazines. Thanks to my editors Mary Ann McGonigle, for her keen eye, and Matthew Kosinski, for his advice and much needed constructive criticism, this would not have been the same without you both. Many thanks to my friends and family, you know who you are! Thank you to my parents, Louis and Linda, for their unconditional love and for teaching me to never give up, which was something I fell back on often during the six years I spent working on this collection of stories. Thanks to my sister Alaina, for who the book is dedicated, I don't know what I would do without you. And finally, special thanks to all my Rutgers friends, for the adventures we shared.

Thank you all!

Also by Joseph Anthony...

The Alphabet of Dating

Remember your first crush, first kiss, first love? Each person holds a special place in your alphabet. We all have an Alphabet of Dating...what does *your* alphabet look like?

* Available at → **diamondmillpress.com** and on **Amazon**

Also Available

An Uneaten Breakfast: Collected Stories and Poems

True Love said to Destiny, "You bring out
the best in me."

* Available at → diamondmillpress.com

www.ingramcontent.com/pod-product-compliance
Lightning Source LLC
Chambersburg PA
CBHW031947170626
46807CB00006B/2385